"Claudia!" Robin Shouted. "Get out of the Way!"

But Claudia stood frozen, like a small, pale statue in the middle of the street.

"Claudia!"

Robin lunged toward the girl and in her panic caught just a glimpse of the driver as the black car bore down relentlessly on top of them.

What she saw paralyzed her . . .

The figure behind the wheel wasn't human.

It stared straight ahead out of black hollow eye sockets, and what little flesh remained on its gleaming skull hung there in long bloody strips.

Robin screamed in horror.

She saw Claudia spread her arms wide . . . step into the path of the car . . . and smile.

Books by Richie Tankersley Cusick

BUFFY, THE VAMPIRE SLAYER
(a novelization based on a screenplay by Joss Whedon)
FATAL SECRETS
HELP WANTED
THE MALL
SILENT STALKER
VAMPIRE

Available from ARCHWAY Paperbacks

RICHIE TANKERSLEY
CUSICK

Help Wanted

AN ARCHWAY PAPERBACK
Published by POCKET BOOKS
New York   London   Toronto   Sydney   Tokyo   Singapore

This book is a work of fiction. Names, characters, places, and incidents are either products of the author's imagination or are used fictitiously. Any resemblance to actual events or locales or persons, living or dead, is entirely coincidental.

AN ARCHWAY PAPERBACK *ORIGINAL*

An Archway Paperback published by
POCKET BOOKS, a division of Simon & Schuster Inc.
1230 Avenue of the Americas, New York, NY 10020

ISBN: 0-671-79403-5

First Archway Paperback printing October 1993

10 9 8 7 6 5 4 3 2 1

AN ARCHWAY PAPERBACK and colophon are registered
trademarks of Simon & Schuster Inc.

Cover art by Gerber Studio

Printed in the U.S.A.

to Barb

for work times and play times . . .
thank you.

Help
Wanted

This is going to be a very weird day." Faye sighed. "I can feel it in the air."

Robin Bailey pushed her tousled brown hair back from her forehead and shifted her books to her other arm. Shivering, she paused at the corner, frowning back at her friend.

"Weird how?"

"Just . . ." Faye shrugged. "I don't know. Weird. Strange things are going to happen. I mean, like this weather. Doesn't it make you feel creepy?"

Robin peered into the drizzly autumn sky. Wet leaves swirled through the air on a gust of cold wind, and the heavy gray clouds threatened more rain.

"It's always like this in October. What's so strange about it?"

"It's this feeling I get—like my skin goes all

prickly and my heart beats fast." Faye paused dramatically and put one hand to her chest. "I got this very same feeling right before Zak broke up with Gina Carmichael and asked *me* to the dance instead of her."

"So that makes you a prophetess?" Robin hid a smile. "And speaking of the dance, don't forget we're supposed to go look for your dress today and—"

"Oh, Robin, I can't!" Faye stopped in her tracks and looked beseechingly at her friend. "Zak asked me out after school! I *have* to go!"

"Faye, you don't have to do anything except die. You don't even have to pay taxes yet." Robin bit her lip and struggled for patience. "You know the dance will be here before you know it, and then you're going to panic because you don't have anything to wear. You can see Zak another time."

"But that's just it, I can't!" Faye's whole body sagged, as if the very thought of being separated from her new boyfriend was more than she could bear. "This is the one day he doesn't have football practice! You don't want me to go back on my promise, do you?"

Robin stared at the other girl. She and Faye had been friends for so long, she could predict every dramatic gesture and exaggerated emotion that Faye could ever think to come up with. She knew a lot of kids found Faye's poise and perfect looks intimidating—that a lot of them wondered why she and Faye were so close—but Robin was the only one who ever stood up to Faye, the only one who could be totally honest and get away with it. Now, as she regarded her friend in tolerant amusement, Robin blinked her blue eyes and tried to keep her voice calm.

"Faye. Ever since you started seeing Zak, you've backed out on a *lot* of promises. All of them to me."

"Well, can I help it if you don't have a boyfriend?" Faye shot back, then immediately looked contrite. "I'm sorry, Robin, I know it's different for you 'cause there's no special guy in your life. But you're my best *friend*. You're supposed to understand these things. Zak is really important to me!"

Robin opened her mouth, then shut it again. She knew it was no use arguing—when Faye had a new love in her life, the rest of the world conveniently ceased to exist.

"Come on," she said, squeezing Faye's elbow. "We're going to be late."

Faye nodded in relief as they hurried across the street and rounded another corner. The bus stop was still four blocks away, and they were already breathless from the raw October chill.

"Still no luck with the Florida trip, huh?" Faye ventured cautiously.

Robin barely glanced at her. "With Brad's college expenses—and Mom going back to school, too—there's just no way she can come up with money for me. Even if it is for the trip of a lifetime."

"But did you tell her Vicki's parents are letting us have the condo for free? For the whole Thanksgiving vacation? All we have to do is buy food—"

"And plane tickets. Of course I told her that. And she really wants me to go, but I have to pay for it myself."

"What about all that money you get from tutoring? And baby-sitting? And helping out in the school office?"

"All that money?" Robin couldn't help laughing. "Yeah, like I get *paid* for helping people with their homework! And I *do* have to buy clothes, you know, and—oh, Faye, there goes the bus!"

Both girls stopped and watched helplessly as the taillights of their school bus faded into the mist far up the street. Faye threw her books down onto the sidewalk and swore loudly.

"Why does this always happen! Every time I spend the night at your house to study, we oversleep and miss the bus, and now we'll get points taken off that *stupid* math test just because we're late—" She broke off abruptly and gave Robin an accusing look. "See? I told you it was going to be a weird day!"

"Faye, every day with you is a weird day. Hurry up—let's cut through Manorwood. It'll be quicker."

Faye had leaned over to retrieve her books and now paused in midstretch to stare at her friend.

"With someone living there now? You really are demented."

4

"No, I'm not. I'm being very sensible, as usual. The hole's still there in the fence—no one's gotten around to fixing it yet. We might as well use it as long as we can."

"Robin, are you out of your mind? The *Swansons* live there now. *Parker* Swanson lives there now. Or have you somehow failed to notice who Parker Swanson is?"

"The new god at Lewis High," Robin said dryly. "How could I miss that?"

He'd been at school nearly two weeks now— and all of Robin's friends could recall the exact moment Parker Swanson had made his grand entrance into their lives. To hear them talk, he was a walking miracle: sun-bleached hair, sea-green eyes, disarming grin, confident walk. The first day he'd breezed into study hall, all the girls had immediately passed around a secret ballot, making bets on who he'd ask out first. It had been a tie between Vicki and Faye, naturally, because they were both beautiful and popular and had that rare and enviable talent for making guys fall head over heels in love with them. Robin's name had been last on the list.

"You're too . . . well, you know . . . serious," Faye had scolded her when the final results were in. "Guys don't like it when you come off like you're judging them."

"I'm not judging them," Robin had argued. "I just think most of them are stupid."

"They are. But you can't let them know you think so."

5

"How can I not let them know? I do homework for half of them now."

Robin would never have admitted it to Faye, but there'd actually been one split second in the beginning when she'd wondered if Parker Swanson might come to her and beg her to help him through English lit. But after just a few days it was clear he'd never be seeking out her tutoring skills. Not only was he always ready with an answer when called upon in class, his answer was always right, and that smile of his never failed to totally charm the teachers.

"If they catch us sneaking around on their property, do you think they'll call the police?" Faye's voice brought Robin back to the present. "I'd hate to miss the math test and get expelled all in the same day."

"We're not sneaking—we're just borrowing one little corner. And people this rich wouldn't bother with the police anyway," Robin said, starting off again. "They'd just have their care-taker shoot us."

Faye burst out laughing and fell into step beside her.

"You mean Skaggs? He couldn't handle any-thing but a beer can and a liquor bottle. Why in the world do you think he's still working here at Manorwood when he's got a job helping the janitor out at school now?"

"Because he needs *lots* of jobs for his drinking money. Plus the fact that he's worked here at Manorwood for years, through *all* the different

6

owners, and in spite of his sleaziness, he still knows the grounds better than anyone else. And he works cheap."

"Gosh"—Faye rolled her eyes—"*I'd* even consider being their groundskeeper if it meant being close to Parker Swanson. I'd give anything to see the inside of the house, wouldn't you? I mean—think about it. Whoever ends up with Parker Swanson gets *everything*—him, his car, his house, his money—"

"His arrogance," Robin cut in. Before Faye could answer, she hurried across another street to where a high iron fence bordered the sidewalk.

Manorwood still stood at the edge of one of the oldest neighborhoods, a venerable and stately reminder of long-ago days when the original estate had included acres of surrounding countryside and town was miles away. The old mansion was perched high on its rocky crag, hidden away behind its fences and private forest, along with a varying succession of reclusive owners. It had been a surprise for everyone, then, when the Swansons moved in, with a son enrolled in the local high school and a maid who actually spoke to people when she did the grocery shopping. Robin supposed she should feel the tiniest bit guilty about trespassing on the new owners, but she and Faye had been taking this shortcut for so many years now, they'd come to consider this corner of Manorwood their own personal thoroughfare.

"Were you really serious about Skaggs shooting us?" Faye whispered.

"Faye," Robin moaned.

"Well, he probably *would* shoot us if he had half a chance. At school he's always scowling at everyone like he hates the human race."

"That's because he's never *been* a member of the human race. He hates anyone who messes things up so he has to work. And anyway, why are you worrying? Skaggs wouldn't be out here now —he'd be at school. He only works here after school and on weekends."

Faye made a face. "What a sleaze. I still think the Swansons could have found someone much more—you know—distinguished—to work for them."

"And you don't think Skaggs is distinguished?" Robin faked surprise. "That classical face—all those pockmarks and scars—his broken nose—the bristles on his chin—"

"Stop! Stop! I'm going to throw up!"

Robin chuckled but couldn't suppress a shudder. "But I agree—he makes my skin crawl. His eyes look right through you. He reminds me of a snake that can't find a rock to crawl under." She gave Faye an impatient push toward the fence. "See anyone around?"

Faye's eyes quickly swept the deserted street and sidewalks. "All clear."

"Great. After you."

Faye worked her way in under a tangled mass

of shrubbery and promptly disappeared through a concealed opening near the bottom of the fence.

"Still all clear. Hand me your stuff."

As Robin shoved her books underneath the bushes and prepared to follow, the sudden blare of a car horn made her straighten up again and turn. A second later a sleek red sports car squealed up onto the curb, promptly spraying her with mud before she could get out of the way.

"Hey!" a voice called smoothly. "Need a ride?"

To Robin's utter dismay, a young man leaned out the window and gave her an easy grin, crossing his tanned arms and sweeping her casually with a pair of startling green eyes.

"You—you—" Robin stared down at her clothes, at the huge globs of mud splattered there. "Look what you've done to my sweater!"

"You *do* go to Lewis High, right?" His voice sounded amused, and as his eyes raked her again from head to foot, Robin felt herself blush furiously. "Fourth period English. You sit in the third row. Right beside that airhead who thinks everything's funny."

This time the blush turned from fury to indignation.

"Her name is Faye, and she happens to be the smartest girl in the whole senior class."

"Next to you, you mean," he corrected with a chuckle. "Come on, get in."

Robin drew herself up stiffly. "No, thank you."

"You're gonna be late."

"So?"

He watched her a moment, his grin widening slowly.

"Suit yourself," he said, and as he roared off again, Robin just managed to avoid being drenched a second time. She was so angry she hardly noticed when the bushes rattled beside her and Faye's head thrust out beneath the dead leaves.

"Robin!" she shrieked. "Do you realize what you've *done!*"

"Yes. Turned down a ride with a total jerk."

"Parker Swanson! That was Parker *Swanson!* In his expensive *car!*"

"Faye"—Robin gave her a withering look—"the guy called you an airhead."

"So it means he noticed me!" Faye wriggled out onto the sidewalk and stood up, brushing herself off excitedly. "He knows who I am! He knows who *you* are! I don't believe this—we could have ridden to school with *Parker Swanson!* Everyone would have been so jealous. He might even have asked me out—before Vicki! I could have touched him!"

"Don't be ridiculous. Come on, I can feel more and more points slipping away on that math test—"

"Well, it's your fault!" Faye still looked slightly stunned. "It's your fault if I don't get asked out before Vicki does, and it's your fault if I flunk that stupid test 'cause I'm late! You should have thought about that, Robin! There are other feelings to consider here besides yours, you know."

Robin sighed, giving Faye a shove toward the shrubbery once more. "Trust me. You're better off without this guy. And what about poor Zak, the love of your life?"

"Just because I'm going with Zak doesn't mean I'm dead," Faye grumbled, but she squeezed back through the fence and pulled Robin in after her. "And by the way, when you tell the girls about this, they're gonna think you made the whole thing up."

"I wasn't planning on telling them."

"Of course we have to tell them! Are you kidding?" Faye shot her an incredulous look as Robin grabbed her arm and gave her a push.

"Faye, come on—if we're late now, it's *your* fault!"

The girls began to run, dodging trees and low-hanging limbs and drifts of dead, soggy leaves. Mist hung in the air like a thin, pale curtain, distorting objects that lay beyond, indistinct, shapeless things crouching in damp shadows. As Robin stumbled over a fallen branch and dropped her books, Faye went on ahead, laughing back at Robin's clumsiness.

"Maybe Parker Swanson was right about you after all," Robin called after her friend.

"What's that?" Faye retorted, still not bothering to stop.

Robin gritted her teeth and pulled one of her notebooks from the mud. She reached for her pen and saw that it was lying in a deep, smudged footprint half filled with water.

Maybe someone else has been using our shortcut.

The thought made Robin uneasy, and she glanced quickly over her shoulder, half expecting someone to jump out at her from the fog.

"I said," Faye's voice called back, startling her, "how was Parker Swanson right about me after all?"

Robin shrugged and wiped her pen off on one leg of her jeans. "About you being an airhead who thinks everything's—"

And then she stopped, her eyes widening, one hand frozen only inches above the ground.

For an endless moment she stared down at her fingertips, and then, slowly, she raised her hand toward her face and gazed at the thick streaks of red running down her fingers and along her open palm.

"Faye!" she cried.

"What is it?" Faye's voice sounded impatient and very faraway.

"Come here!"

Robin's gaze dropped once more to the ground. She saw the wide rut worn through the leaves—as though something heavy had been dragged there—and the dark red swashes, thick and jellylike swirled in the mud . . .

And as she reached out, trembling, to brush some leaves away, she saw the splintered twigs and bits of broken pinecones, all tangled together with clumps of dark hair.

2

For one long horrified moment Robin couldn't do anything but stare. She didn't even realize Faye had come up behind her until she heard the other girl's squeal at her back.

Faye gasped. "What *is* that?"

"I . . . I don't know . . ." Robin looked up at her friend in dismay. "I slipped and dropped my books and . . ."

"Is that *blood?*"

"It looks like—"

"And *hair?*"

"Well . . . I . . ."

"Cover it up before I get sick!"

Hastily Robin brushed the leaves back in place, nearly falling again as she tried to scramble up.

Faye grabbed her arm to steady her. "Are you okay?"

"Are you?" Robin's eyes were still riveted on that flattened trail in the leaves. It led off for several yards, then angled off through a dense grove of pines, disappearing beneath shadows and fog. "What are we going to do?" she murmured.

"Do?" Faye stared at her blankly. "What do you mean?"

"I mean—do we tell the Swansons about this?"

"About what? Trespassing?"

"Or do we go to the police?" Robin rushed on. "Should one of us stay here while the other gets help?"

"Why?" Faye's look turned slightly incredulous. "What are you talking about?"

Robin gazed at her friend a moment, then frowned. "Faye, am I missing something here? Or did you just see what I saw?"

"Some marks on the ground." Faye jabbed a finger downward. "Some hair—"

"Faye—" Robin began, but the other girl cut her off.

"Robin, what's the matter with you? Do you think the Swansons even care if some poor animal gets killed on their property? Skaggs probably shoots anything on four legs and eats it for breakfast."

"Animal?" This time it was Robin's turn to look surprised. "You think this was an . . . animal?"

"Well, what did *you* think it was?"

Faye held her friend's eyes for a long moment, then began slowly shaking her head.

"Oh, Robin . . . come on, now . . ."

"But—that blood—and—and—the hair—"

"Let's not stop to think about the details of the struggle, okay?" Faye made a face. "Survival of the fittest, Robin, remember? I bet it was a raccoon and some dogs. Raccoons are always coming around raiding our garbage cans, and Dad won't let us near them. He says they're really mean fighters."

Robin was still staring at the indentation in the leaves. Faye grabbed her sleeve and shook it.

"Come on—I'd like to at least *try* to pass that math test this morning, okay? Please?"

Robin gave a vague nod and followed as her friend hurried away. Faye was right, of course, she argued with herself—those smears of blood and that hair had only been the remains of some unfortunate animal. What had she been thinking of, anyway?

But that path through the leaves . . . it was so wide . . . so mashed down . . . that dead animal would had to have been awfully big. . . .

With a sheer act of will Robin forced the suspicions from her mind and ran to catch up with Faye. By the time they reached school, they'd already missed homeroom, so after a quick stop at the office, the girls dashed into math class, receiving a warning glare from Mrs. Grouse as they collected their tests. Breathing a sigh of relief, Robin slipped into her desk and caught a wink from the long-haired boy slouched next to her.

"You lead a charmed life, Bailey," Walt murmured under his breath.

Robin smiled and lowered her head, trying to concentrate on her test paper. No one ever called Theodore Waltermize by his real name. Tall and soft-spoken, Walt was an enigma Robin hadn't been able to figure out even though he'd transferred to Lewis High at the start of the school year. He wasn't handsome in that breathtaking way Parker Swanson was, yet there was something equally intriguing about him—his sandy hair, for one thing, hanging thick and wavy past his shoulders; his customary outfit of threadbare jeans and faded workshirt; the steady calm of his brown eyes; and his square stubborn jaw. She knew a lot of girls were attracted to him, because he was a main topic of fantasizing at lunch and sleepovers and in the girls' locker room—and yet she never saw Walt with a date or even hanging out much with the other guys. A lot of her friends thought he was a brain, and therefore unapproachable, and some suspected he was really a narc because his uncle used to work on the local police force, but Robin thought that maybe he was just shy. Now, as she risked a glance in Walt's direction, she saw that he was still watching her, and she dropped her eyes back to her paper.

Time passed too quickly. Before she'd quite managed to finish the math test, Robin heard the bell ring, and she hastily scribbled a guess to the last problem. The room had already emptied by the time she handed in her paper. She went out glumly and found Faye waiting for her in the hall.

"So what'd you think?" Faye ran one hand back through her bleached hair and tossed her head, model-style. "Did you know anything?"

"Foreign language." Robin sighed. "Come on. I've got to stop at my locker."

"Me, too. We should have just taken our time this morning. Saved Mrs. Grouse the trouble of flunking us."

Faye's locker was right beneath Robin's at the very end of the hall. While Faye knelt on the floor and began pulling out an impossible stash of books and papers, Robin wandered across the corridor, to the gigantic bulletin board on the wall. There was likely to be *anything* posted here—as Robin's eyes traveled slowly across the hodgepodge of clutter, she saw personal messages, cartoons, and drawings; official announcements from the teachers and the principal; poems and quotes for the day; schedules of club meetings and sports events; newspaper and magazine clippings; even telephone numbers. A girl had lost her purse in the cafeteria. Someone was offering baby-sitting services; another needed tutoring in biology. Someone else had found an earring and hung it on a push pin. There were a bunch of faded photographs from the last class picnic—one of Vicki in her too-tight sweatshirt —another of Faye eating a hotdog—Walt alone, leaning against a tree—plus one of herself smiling that she had no idea who had taken.

And then she saw the ad.

It had been ripped from the morning paper and was practically buried beneath the photographs, yet the bold black print seemed to speak just to her:

HELP WANTED

GET RICH QUICK

DETAIL-ORIENTED STUDENT FOR CATALOGING
    PERSONAL LIBRARY

NO EXPERIENCE NECESSARY

555-4357

Robin's heart leapt, yet she forced herself to go back and read the ad through one more time. Detail work and books—two things she loved! An absolute dream job, it sounded like—*so of course someone's probably snatched it up by now—just my luck.* . . . Still, it couldn't hurt to call and find out. She pulled the paper off the bulletin board and stuck it in her pocket just as Faye came up juggling an armload of notebooks.

"Have you seen Vicki?" Faye frowned. "Is she sick or something?"

Robin stopped and thought a minute. "She's always sick when there's a math test. You know that."

"Well, she'd better show up sometime today," Faye grumbled. "She was supposed to bring back that bracelet I loaned her. The little thief."

"Why is she a thief if you loaned it to her?"

"Because she'll keep conveniently leaving it at home until I forget about it."

"Then don't forget about it."

"Well, I have so much on my mind!" Faye complained. "I can't remember *everything* that's important!"

"How about which class you have this hour," Robin deadpanned. "Social studies? Gym? Just blink once for yes, twice for no."

She opened her mouth to say more, but Faye grabbed her arm and hustled her off to class.

Robin could hardly wait for three-fifteen. Faye had been quick to spread the word about their morning encounter with Parker Swanson, and all day long Robin had had to endure glances of half envy, half disbelief from her female classmates. She supposed she should have been flattered by all the curious attention, but today it only irritated her, and when Parker made a point of waving at her in English class, she slid down in her seat, all too conscious of every girl in the room staring.

She'd forgotten about some overdue library books she had to return. By the time she discovered them in her locker and dropped them off, she'd missed the bus again and resigned herself to walking home. She couldn't remember the weather ever being this cold in October before. Robin hurried through the old, silent neighborhoods and huddled deep into her jacket, keeping a nervous eye on the lengthening shadows around her. It had started getting dark so early now; she hated going home in near-twilight. As she passed the gates of Manorwood, an image of those blood-soaked leaves flashed into her mind, and she quickened her steps. *Only an animal . . . of course it was . . . what else could it have been . . . ?*

"This is going to be a weird day . . . strange things are going to happen. . . ."

Robin began to run. She could still hear Faye's premonition, and she tried fiercely to block it out. *What's wrong with you—quit being so silly.* Yet it was only when she reached the warmth of her own house that she finally began to relax.

"Mom?"

Robin's voice echoed back to her from empty rooms. After a quick inspection of the downstairs, she remembered her mother had class tonight after work and wouldn't be home till late. At times like this she really missed her older brother and wished he hadn't gone away to college. At times like this she wished her parents hadn't gotten a divorce, that Mom didn't have to work and hadn't decided to go back to school, that Dad hadn't remarried and moved halfway around the world. She could remember a time when the house hadn't been empty and cold. She could even remember a time when they hadn't had to worry about money. . . .

Angrily Robin yanked the receiver off the kitchen phone and pulled the crumpled ad from her pocket. When the voice spoke on the other end of the line, she was already bracing herself to be disappointed.

"Hello?" A man's voice. He sounded old.

"Yes . . ." Robin stammered. "Yes . . . I'm . . . I'm calling about the ad."

There was a moment of silence, and Robin's heart sank into her stomach.

"The ad about the job—the personal library." She took a deep breath and plunged on. "It's probably already been taken, hasn't it? I'm sorry—I just thought I'd check and—"

"No," the voice sounded mildly surprised. "No. It's not taken."

"It isn't? Really?"

"No. As a matter of fact, you're the first one to call."

"I am?" She switched the receiver to her other hand and wiped her sweaty palm on her shirt. *Come on, Robin, try to be professional.* "Well, I really thought the job sounded interesting. Could you tell me a little more about it?"

This time the voice sounded crotchety. "I could if I felt like it. But it might make more sense if you came in person. What's your name?"

"My name?"

"You have a name, don't you? If I have to interview you, I have to know what to call you, don't I?"

"Oh. Yes. Robin Bailey."

"Robin Bailey," the voice repeated. "You're a student?"

"Yes. A senior."

"Can you come at seven?"

"You mean tonight?"

"What's wrong with tonight?"

"Well . . . nothing." *Three hours from now.* Robin's mind raced. "Will the interview take long?"

"Depends on how long you want to stay."

"Oh. Not long, probably."

"Then there's your answer."

What am I getting myself into? Robin glanced at the kitchen clock. Mom wouldn't be home till nearly ten-thirty; there'd be plenty of time to go for an interview and be back before then.

"Seven would be fine," she said.

"Fine for me, too. Sixty-five sixty-five Wald Avenue."

"Wait—I'm writing it down." Robin scribbled on a notepad, then stared at the numbers, frowning. They seemed familiar, but before she could figure out why, the voice went on again.

"Hope you don't scare easy," it said.

"What?"

The line went dead. Robin stared at the receiver, then quickly hung it up.

What a crazy conversation—if I had any brains at all, I'd forget about this whole thing and not go tonight.

She leaned against the kitchen sink and stared out the window. Going for a job interview was one thing—going alone after dark to a total stranger's house was another thing altogether. *Especially when he sounds like a mental case.*

23

Mom would be furious when she found out—
how many times had she lectured Robin on what
could happen to a teenage girl alone in the wrong
place at the wrong time?

But I'm not a child, Robin argued with herself.
*I'm doing something responsible, I'm going for an
interview so I can make money to do something I
really want, and everyone's been able to do what
they want but me, and I deserve this. So I'm going.*

Mind made up, she straightened with a fierce
resolve, then paced the floor and watched the
clock. Wald Avenue wasn't that far—in fact, it
was on the very route she walked back and forth
to school. Robin knew the general location—
how dangerous could it be going to the house of a
neighbor?

At six-thirty she started off briskly, hands
clenched in her pockets. Her shoes echoed eerily
on the pavement, sharp stabbing sounds, and the
wind, whining through the bare trees, gusted at
her back, forcing her along. Once she thought she
heard footsteps, but when she looked back over
her shoulder, the sidewalk was empty and dark.
Some of the streetlights had gone out, plunging
the curbs and yards into pockets of deep shadow.

At last she reached the corner and saw the
street sign above her—Wald Avenue. She began
searching for house numbers, but after going the
length of the block, she stopped in dismay. The
street numbers seemed to jump, completely
missing 6565. *As if the house doesn't even
exist. . . .*

Robin set her jaw and stopped. Methodically she went back to the opposite end of the block and started over again, just to make sure she hadn't missed it. Still no 6565.

That's it, I'm going home.

Feeling foolish for having started out at all, Robin paused beneath a sputtering lamppost to tie her shoe. Across the street Manorwood's black iron fence hid the house and grounds from view, its spiked gates silhouetted against the night sky. A blast of wind fanned the tree branches that overhung the fence, and as it did, a frail beam of moonlight filtered down, illuminating the peeling street numbers above the gate.

6565.

Robin's heart fluttered into her stomach.

She was hardly aware of moving across the street . . . hardly aware of stopping beside the gate as her eyes remained fixed on those numbers high above her head.

Something rustled in the shrubbery on the other side of the fence.

There was a muffled thudding sound . . . like footsteps running away . . .

Robin lifted one hand toward the gate.

"Come in," a voice said, right beside her.

Robin whirled with a gasp, but no one was there.

3

"Come in," the disembodied voice said again. *A man's voice . . . the voice on the phone . . .* "The gate's open."

Robin stared, her skin going cold. Before her eyes, the gate began to swing inward, leaving just enough space to squeeze through. As her frightened eyes swept the shadows on the other side of the fence, the voice spoke again, impatiently.

"I can see you on the security camera, and the gate works on remote. Don't be so jumpy! Just follow the driveway to the house and come in the front door."

Now's my chance, Robin thought wildly. *Now's my chance to turn and run before I make an even bigger fool of myself.* The memory of Parker Swanson and her refusal to ride with him still burned in her mind. Suppose this was some kind of weird joke, some strange retaliation for having snubbed him this morning. . . . *He'd be just the type to hold a grudge when his pride was hurt.* . . .

And yet curiosity got the better of her. The thought of actually seeing the inside of the house after admiring it for all these years . . . the irresistible temptation of that ad . . .

Robin forced all suspicions from her mind and started up the wide, curving drive. She followed it for quite a way up a thickly wooded incline, relieved when she reached the house at last.

Manorwood stood there, haughty and proud, elegant even in the fog. It was a strange piece of property—during one of its ownerless interims, Robin and Faye had gone exploring and found its thick forests riddled with dangerous ravines, the property itself bordered on one side by cliffs that overhung the dry, rocky riverbed far below. But tonight it didn't look dangerous at all. Tonight lights gleamed softly from windows on every floor, casting long shadows over the surrounding trees and lawns, and the curved drive beside the porch was occupied by a limousine and Parker's sports car.

The front door was standing wide open.

This is really crazy—what am I doing here?

Robin stood at the bottom of the porch steps. She stared up at the magnificent house, took a deep breath, and turned to go back when a voice stopped her.

"Robin Bailey, get in here. It's too damp to keep this door open."

The peculiar little man was very short and very

stooped—a fairy-tale troll in a maroon dressing gown much too big and long for his size. Bushy white hair stuck out all around his bald spot and both of his ears, and white bushy brows sat low over his eyes. Because of his hunched shape, he didn't seem able to lift his head much higher than his shoulders, and as he motioned Robin through the door, his chin moved back and forth in a sideways sort of nod. He was scowling at her, and as Robin glanced down at his feet, she saw that he was wearing big fuzzy purple house slippers.

"Didn't your mother ever teach you not to gawk?" he said, wagging his head at her again. "Just let me get this blasted door shut, and then you can gawk at me in the light, if you must!"

Robin hadn't meant to stare, but she couldn't help it. As the old man slammed the door and turned to face her, she lowered her eyes quickly.

"Not what you expected, eh?" the old man burst out at her. "Well, I never am what most people expect. Come on. This way."

Again he waved one arm at her and promptly began shuffling across the wide foyer. Robin glanced toward the locked door and realized she had no choice now but to follow. She saw her host disappear through a wide archway off the entrance hall, and she went cautiously after him.

She had never seen such a beautiful room. Spacious and satiny and luxurious, every detail of the furniture, the mirrors, the bookcases, and the statuary spoke of money, and yet Robin stood there feeling cold and horribly out of place. She felt as if she'd walked into a magazine ad where real people never lived, and as her eyes swept up to the friezes on the ceiling, she had to forcibly restrain herself not to turn and run. *I don't belong here. . . . Why did I come . . . ?*

"Well, Robin Bailey," the little man began, then to her surprise, turned to her with a chuckle. "You are Robin Bailey, aren't you? What a joke on me if you're not! What if you came to rob the place, and I simply invited you in! Although"— he narrowed his eyes at her—"you don't look as if you could carry much."

He jerked his chin in the direction of a velvet sofa, and after a slight hesitation, Robin sat down, all too conscious of her muddy sneakers. When she looked up again, the old man had positioned himself next to the fireplace on the opposite wall and was once more watching her with narrowed eyes.

"So what would you like to know, Robin Bailey?"

Swallowing hard, Robin tried to think of something half intelligent to say.

"Are you . . . are you Mr. Swanson?" she asked at last. The idea of this funny little man being Parker's father was almost more than she could take.

"I am the *eldest* Mr. Swanson. I am the *patriarch* Mr. Swanson. I am Hercules Diffenbach Swanson." His eyes flashed. "There's me, my stupid son, Gardner, and my brilliant grandson, Parker."

"I . . ." Robin shook her head. "I . . . I'm sorry. I knew that your family had moved in here—I mean, everyone had heard that—but I didn't know about . . . you."

"Of course not. I'm the *eccentric* Swanson. The one no one ever talks about. They keep me chained up in the attic, you know. I've only just broken out this afternoon."

Robin's eyes widened. Mr. Swanson stared at her a full minute, then burst out laughing.

"I'm *kidding*, Robin Bailey—it's a joke! Of course they don't chain me up—they'd have their hands full if they ever tried such a thing— you can put that in your pipe and smoke it!"

Robin squirmed and glanced out into the hall. She wondered if she could make it to the front door and get it unlocked before Mr. Swanson came after her.

"So," he said, picking up a poker, stabbing at the fire. "You think you'd like this job, do you? Well, I think you would, too. I've done some checking on you."

"On . . . on me?"

"Of course on you. Why would I check on someone else if you're the one who wants to work here?" He took one jab at a log, and it promptly dissolved into hissing sparks. "My grandson had quite a lot to say about you, Robin Bailey."

"Your . . ." She felt her voice die. She cleared her throat and tried again. "I don't even know Parker, Mr. Swanson. I mean, well, I know who he is, and—"

"And you have English literature together every afternoon," the man continued, nodding emphatically. "But he knows quite a lot about *you*, young lady. Enough to convince me you'd be perfect for this job."

"Excuse me, Mr. Swanson, but really, I—"

"He said you were smart. Smartest in the senior class, was what he said."

"Well, no, actually—"

"And popular. With girls *and* boys. Truthful. Helpful. Kind, he said. And unpretentious. Can you imagine that—Parker knowing what unpretentious is! Kid thinks he's God's gift to women!"

Robin's mouth dropped open.

"You agree with me, too," Mr. Swanson said triumphantly. "But that's neither here nor there. Important thing is, I believe him, what he says about you. And he wasn't wrong, either, saying you're pretty."

Robin felt her cheeks flame. She stared at the floor and tried to tuck one sneaker behind the other leg of her jeans.

"And modest," Mr. Swanson added. "I like that. Now, look here, Robin Bailey, I need someone I can count on—depend on. And I think you're just the one for—"

"Excuse me, sir," a voice interrupted from the doorway, "but I didn't hear the doorbell ring."

"Because it *didn't!*" Mr. Swanson clasped his hands behind his back and bent forward at a forty-five degree angle. "Because Robin here

31

didn't *ring* it! Because I was right there waiting for her when she *got* here!"

To Robin's dismay he threw a big wink back at her over his shoulder and looked immensely pleased with himself.

"This is Robin Bailey, Winifred." He waved one arm vaguely in Robin's direction. "She's come about the advertisement I had Parker put up in his school today."

There was a slight movement from the shadows beyond the threshold, and Robin saw a woman step forward into the light. She was tall and straight and rather prim and looked very much like the plain old broom she was holding.

"Shall I get refreshments?" she asked, and Mr. Swanson deferred to his guest with a nod.

"No, thanks," Robin said quickly. "Nothing for me."

"Then get out of here, Winifred," Mr. Swanson said. He flapped his arms wildly toward the woman, but she merely turned without the slightest show of alarm at his behavior.

"If you need me—"

"Yes, yes, we'll call you," Mr. Swanson shouted after her impatiently. "Well and good, Winifred, well and good." He glanced over at Robin and chuckled, affording her a loud stage whisper. "Winifred's been with us for years. Thinks she runs the place—*and* us! Thinks we can't do without her. Well, we can't! But I won't *tell* her that! Don't want her getting a big head!"

Robin looked down at the floor and sighed.

"Please, Mr. Swanson—"

"Don't call me Mr. Swanson. Makes me feel old. Call me Herk."

"But—Mr.—I mean, Herk—"

"A hundred dollars a week," he announced. "Does that suit you?"

"A hundred . . ." Robin nearly choked, but the old man rushed on.

"I see it does. Good! 'Get rich quick'—wasn't that what the ad said? That was *my* idea. 'Get rich quick'—catchy, huh? Well, it caught *you,* and I'm glad. A hundred dollars, Robin Bailey. That'll make the job more tempting. You'll need all the stamina you can muster."

"Stamina? You mean because the job is demanding? I don't mind hard work. I do tutoring and I also help out in the school administration—"

"Not stamina for the job. Stamina to deal with this nutty family! Look here."

Robin looked. Herk fairly skittered over to a wall of small mahogany doors and began to open them, one by one. In each compartment there were books, books, and more books, and boxes stacked one on top of the other, all of them neatly labeled but unreadable from where Robin sat.

"See this?" Herk barked.

Robin nodded.

"These are Lillith's things." His eyes narrowed, as though he were angry about something. "Her books. Tons of them. Millions of them."

"Lillith?" Robin echoed, but he rushed on.

"All these"—he indicated the whole wall of cupboards with a sweep of his hand—"are being donated to the local library here. But before we can give the blasted things away, they need to be appraised. And before the appraiser can come, they need to be cataloged. If it were up to me, I'd dump the whole caboodle in the fireplace and have done with them! But it's not up to me! 'Cause I'm old! No one cares to hear *my* opinion!"

He stopped. He leaned over even farther and yanked one book from its shelf, rifling haphazardly through its pages.

"This one's art. But I don't know what all's in the rest. Nonsense and whatnot. Think you can handle it?"

Robin nodded. The old man flashed her a grim smile, then jerked to attention.

"What was that?" he said sharply. "Did you hear something?"

Robin jumped in her seat. She watched as Herk's eyes quickly scanned the room and finally stopped at the far wall, where a set of French doors stood slightly ajar. Filmy white curtains fanned in on the night breeze, and Robin glimpsed what might have been a shadowy patio lying beyond.

"What?" Robin whispered.

Herk had gone stiff and silent. He held one finger to his lips, but after a moment he lowered his hand again and shook his head.

"Thought I heard something. Did *you* hear something?"

"N-no."

"Crazy house. Crazy family," Herk muttered. "Some of these books are falling apart, they're so old. You don't have to be careful with them—I just want the job done. Want to get them out of here. Family won't do it. They're all insane." He straightened and replaced the book, then slammed the cabinet door.

"Well . . ." Robin ventured cautiously, "will Lillith be working with me? To tell me exactly what she wants me to say about the books?"

"Don't see how she can!" he snorted.

"Oh." Robin nodded again. "Oh. So . . . will I meet her?"

"Meet her?" Herk echoed. As Robin watched, his eyes narrowed and swung toward the door. "There she is," he muttered. "You can meet her now."

Automatically Robin turned. She could see the walls and the archway and the foyer beyond that, and the lights glowing softly all around. But besides the strange little man by the fireplace, there was no one else in the room.

"Where?" she asked uneasily. "I don't see her."

"There. Just behind you."

A sudden draft swept through the room, so piercingly cold that Robin caught her breath. She could see the French doors shivering and the darkened patio crouched outside and the curtains billowing like restless phantoms on the chilled autumn wind. And as her eyes struggled to focus on the night beyond, she could swear she saw something else—*something moving*—for just the briefest instant—a subtle thickening, then fading of the darkness . . .

Robin gasped and jumped to her feet, turning again toward the hall door.

She hadn't noticed the portrait when she'd first come in. Even though it was quite large, it hung inconspicuously to one side of the arch, positioned within a niche, hiding from the light. Now, as Herk continued to gaze at it, Robin started forward, half fascinated, half repulsed by what she saw.

The woman was delicate and childlike, her small face ghostly pale and painfully vulnerable. Long blond hair streamed out like wings around her head and shoulders, and her clear violet eyes gazed wide with some unknown horror. She wore a beautiful white robe, yet it hung in shreds from her fragile body—the sleeves, the skirt, the bodice slashed and torn, smeared and stained with blood. Her right hand plunged a knife deep into her breast. She was smiling.

"My God . . ." Robin murmured, but before

she could say anything more, Herk spoke out from the shadows behind her.

"She always had a fear she would die violently."

Robin couldn't make herself face him. "And did she?"

"Oh, yes. She killed herself."

4

Robin couldn't take her eyes from the painting. The face was so innocent, yet at the same time so filled with pain and unspoken terror. . . .

"She was an artist, you know," Herk went on, his scowl deepening. "And that was her favorite —that self-portrait. It shakes people up, but I like it there. Just to remind me she's really gone."

"But . . . how can you . . . it's so . . ." Robin's voice trailed away, but Herk picked up her thoughts.

"You think I'm mean. Mean and cruel and insensitive. Well, I'm not, Robin Bailey. She was an evil woman, and she never should have married my son. She got exactly what she deserved."

Robin didn't want to hear any more. She glanced longingly toward the door, but Herk kept on.

"She was the second Mrs. Swanson. Married

Gardner after his first wife died. *Against my wishes,* I might add! Nothing good came from *that* match. As if Lillith weren't bad enough, Claudia moved right in with her—along with the suitcases and all these damn books."

Robin was getting more confused by the minute.

"Who's Claudia" she murmured.

"Lillith's daughter." Herk's face darkened. "Creepy kid. She *should* be in school now, but she's still grieving, is what the doctor said. Lillith's been dead nearly six months now, and Claudia still can't get over it."

Robin heard the irritation in his voice and finally turned around.

"But—I mean—it *is* her mother who died—"

"Don't give me that sad old mother-daughter bonding stuff—they fought like two cats over a saucer of cream! Couldn't stand each other when Lillith *was* alive—can't see why Claudia's so broken up over her now."

He hobbled over to the portrait and studied it silently for several seconds. Robin gave it one more reluctant glance, then dropped her eyes. Her heart felt immeasurably sad.

"How—how did she die?" Robin spoke at last.

"Messy. Very messy." Herk shook his head. "Slit her wrists and threw herself into the ocean. Wanted to make sure it worked one way or the other, I guess."

Robin stared at him, wishing she'd never asked.

"Thing is, she must have changed her mind at the end. Changed her mind and started calling for help. Fishermen bringing in their boats heard her. Said she was calling Claudia's name. It was windy that night, and stormy. By the time they got help out there, Lillith was gone. It was Claudia who finally found her—later on—washed up on the beach."

"You mean—Claudia saw her after it happened?"

"Horrible sight. You ever see anyone drowned? Been in the water a long time? Course, she'd practically bled to death before she jumped—"

"Jumped?"

"Off the cliff!" Herk sounded impatient. "She cut herself, and then she jumped! I remember like it was yesterday. Body ended up in a little cove near our house, and Claudia just standing there on the rocks screaming and screaming."

Robin closed her eyes, feeling suddenly queasy. "Oh, that poor girl. It must have been so horrible for her."

"Went all to pieces. Of course, she always *was* a strange little thing. But after that . . ." Herk lifted one bushy brow. "Hasn't been dealing with a full deck, if you know what I mean."

Robin said nothing. She told herself she wouldn't look at the painting again, yet she felt her eyes lift helplessly, felt herself gazing at the beautiful, tortured face and feeling so sorry.

"Secretly you're wanting to know why Lillith

did it." Herk gave her a look that was almost smug. "But you're too polite to ask."

"No. It's none of my—"

"It's always like that with suicide, isn't it? Wanting to know—but *not* wanting to. We see ourselves in those poor doomed creatures. We see ourselves and the times we've needed a way out, and we can't help but wonder . . . was it worth it for them? Did it solve what they hoped it would? Or do they wish they were back here . . . with the same set of problems to face?" He stared at her a long moment. "Do you believe the dead come back, Robin Bailey? Especially . . . the evil ones?"

"I have to go," Robin said abruptly. She forced herself to move through the doorway and out into the entrance hall.

"So you'll take the job?" Herk asked.

"I . . ." Suddenly Robin wanted to say no, to say goodbye, to say she would never come near Manorwood ever again. But instead she heard herself speaking, as from a long way off. "I'll think about it."

"See that you do. See that you show up here right after school." He accompanied her to the door and stood there just inside the threshold as she went past him out onto the porch. She glanced back and he was nodding at her, and his face broke into an impish smile that was somehow tinged with a remote sadness.

"Tomorrow," he said to her, and he lifted his hand in a salute. "You're needed here."

Robin stared out into the darkness. A dozen excuses swirled through her brain, but when she turned back to face him, Herk had closed the door, leaving her alone on the steps.

That's it. That's the last time I ever answer some ad from some newspaper. He's crazy and the job is crazy and the whole family's probably crazier than he is. . . .

Robin hurried back down the driveway. With every few steps she glanced over her shoulder at the silhouette of the house growing smaller and hazier through the trees. The night seemed darker than ever out here in the woods, and the fog had thickened so much, she could hardly see the twists and turns of the drive stretching out ahead of her. Surely the entrance couldn't be much farther—it hadn't seemed to take this long between the house and the main gates before. Without warning, a flash of memory came back to her—she saw herself taking the shortcut that morning, slipping in the mud, finding that bloody trench through the leaves. Her heart thudded in her chest, and she began to run. *Only an animal . . . that's all it was . . . only some poor animal . . .*

She didn't actually see the shadowy figure step out onto the drive in front of her—didn't actually see it slip silently from the fog and stand there, waiting.

Only when she was practically on top of it did Robin finally realize that something was blocking her path—and as she felt the impact of a body against hers, as she felt the arms clamp around her, such a wave of terror struck that she couldn't even scream.

"Well, now," a voice hissed. "Why you runnin' so fast?"

She knew that voice.

Even in her paralyzed state, Robin knew that voice, for she'd heard it hundreds of times at school, on the campus, in the gym, in the maintenance room. She'd have known it even if it hadn't been thick with cigarette smoke and liquor, and as awareness began to seep into her brain, she also felt his breath on the side of her neck.

"Let me go!"

At last Robin was able to move, and as she twisted in his grasp and thrashed out at him, Roy Skaggs fell back and staggered several steps.

Robin's hands were raised, ready to swing again, but the man shook his head and grinned a lopsided grin.

"I know you," he slurred. His grin widened, and he pointed with one limp arm. "Hey—I know you!"

"Don't you ever touch me again." Robin was seething. "If you do, I'm going to report you to the police."

"You can't do nothin'," he countered, his tone smug. "I work here, and you can't do nothin'. I belong here."

"I don't think Mr. Swanson would like hearing how you attack his guests." Robin fought to keep her voice steady. "Or how drunk you are. And I don't think the school would like to hear about it, either."

"I didn't know it was you," Skaggs said, his voice sinking to a whine. "Honest. I didn't know. I was just keepin' out intruders. I thought you was tryin' to rob the place. Sneakin' around like that—"

"I wasn't sneaking. If you ever try anything like that again, I'll—"

"Go 'head." His lips curled in a snarl. "And I'll hurt you, little girl. You hear? Miss High-and-Mighty? I can and I will. So don't go gettin' any ideas."

"Get out of my way," Robin said icily.

She could see the gate now, looming at the end of the drive, and she pushed past him and raced toward it.

"You better run!" Skaggs yelled behind her. "You listen to me!"

Robin clamped her hands over her ears, trying to shut out the sound of his voice, but still she could hear him shouting at the top of his lungs.

"You better run, little girl, far away from this place! You better run for your *life!*"

5

You look kind of pale this morning." Faye eyed Robin critically as they headed across the school-yard. "Did you sleep okay?"

"Not really," Robin admitted and was almost glad when Faye started rambling on and on about being with Zak the day before.

She *wanted* to tell Faye what had happened last night, how she'd finally gotten home from Manorwood and been a nervous wreck the rest of the evening, how she couldn't stop thinking about that woman in the portrait or the strange girl named Claudia. . . .

She'd *wanted* to tell her mother everything, too, had *started* to tell her a hundred different times, but something had held Robin back. Partly because she knew Mom wouldn't want her taking a job in a strange tragic household like that; partly because she hadn't been able to stop thinking about the hundred dollars a week. *The trip to Florida and new clothes, too—and such easy money!* Just sitting there going through boxes and shelves and making lists of books! Robin had finally told her mother *half* the truth —that she was working for a nice old man who needed his library put in order—and after Mom realized it was the Swanson family, she'd been too impressed to ask a lot of questions. Then Robin had gone directly up to bed, but she hadn't been able to sleep. Her stomach had been in knots all night, and she'd tossed until the alarm went off this morning.

The whole thing was weird, she'd told herself as she got ready for school. *Too weird.* There was a feeling about it she couldn't seem to shake, an uneasiness she couldn't get rid of. That whole suicide thing, and Herk's obvious hatred for Lillith, and why hadn't Parker ever mentioned his sister to anyone? To Robin's knowledge, none of the other kids had ever heard of Claudia Swanson, or she was sure someone would have said something. And then there was Skaggs, of course. He'd frightened her badly, that was part of it—*but he was drunk. He'll never remember a thing about it today.*

She wondered what Claudia looked like, how old she was, when she'd be able to meet her in person.

And she thought about Parker.

If I take that job, I'll be in that house, I'll be where Parker is, I'll get to know Claudia, and I'll find out what really goes on inside the walls of Manorwood, and I'll make tons of money in the process. . . .

"Did you hear me?" Faye jostled her. "You look like you're a million miles away."

"Oh. Sorry. I'm—"

"Look. There's Parker."

Faye's voice ended on a breathless note, and Robin tried to look without being obvious. Parker was standing near the outside stairs, sharing a joke with the rest of the guys crowded around him.

Faye sighed again and nudged Robin with her elbow.

"I want a date with him. Please, God."

As the girls passed by, Faye swung into her most seductive walk, and Robin steeled herself as whistles serenaded them into the building.

"Why do you do that?" she muttered. "It's so embarrassing."

"No, it's not." Faye giggled. "And I do it because I'm good at it."

Faye let go of the door before she realized Robin hadn't quite crossed the threshold. Robin, struggling with her books, glanced up just in time to see the door swinging into her face.

Faye moaned. "He's so gorgeous. Honestly, Robin, sometimes I think—*Robin!*"

Robin managed to catch herself before she'd fully hit the floor. As her books spilled out helter-skelter, she went down on her knees and swore loudly at the pain. She felt her stockings rip and felt herself being squashed in the doorway and caught just a glimpse of Faye turning back for her. And then suddenly someone else was there, wedging open the door and pulling her to her feet.

"Rule number one. Never use your face for a doorstop."

Flustered, Robin looked up into Parker's wide grin. She could hear jokes and laughter as students pushed past them, and Parker steered her clumsily to one side of the hall.

"You okay?" He propped her against the wall and glanced back as Faye came rushing up. "If you'd been watching where you were going instead of watching me—"

"I was not watching you!" Robin said angrily. She wished she could disappear. She wished she could just say a magic word and wake up to find her total humiliation was only a nightmare. But instead she looked helplessly at Faye as her friend peered into her face.

"Ewww! You're bleeding!" Faye squealed.

"I am?"

While Faye rummaged through her purse, Robin put one hand to her face and felt a warm trickle of blood across her lips. She started to say something when Faye slammed a tissue against her mouth, making her moan instead.

"Oh, that's great, Faye." Parker chuckled. "I like that cute squashed look."

—"I'm helping her," Faye said indignantly. "I *know* what I'm doing, thank you very—"

"Can we go?" Robin broke in. "Please? We're holding up traffic."

Parker barely glanced at the curious onlookers streaming by in the corridor. "What do you mean, can you go? Do you realize how *popular* you are just because I'm standing here beside you?"

"You are such a jerk!" Robin burst out.

As Parker pressed her back against the wall, she saw Walt sauntering by, that faint look of amusement on his face.

"You sure know how to make a great impression, Bailey," he greeted her and continued on down the hall.

"That's it," Robin said. "I'm going."

But before she could move, Parker took her chin in his hand and angled her head back. Faye didn't say a word; all she could do was stare.

"I hear," Parker murmured, "that you and I might be seeing quite a lot of each other."

Startled, Robin looked straight into his eyes. *So green . . . I've never seen eyes so green. . . .* It seemed to take all her effort to look away again. She glanced over at Faye, but the other girl looked hypnotized.

"Lucky you," Parker whispered.

"Go start your own fan club," Robin said, giving him a shove. "I've got to go to my locker."

Again she tried to get away, but his fingers tightened ever so slowly on her chin, holding it firmly in place. Unnerved, she felt her gaze drawn back to his. For one split second it was as if she had no will of her own, as though she'd lost all sense of her surroundings, all sense of everything except the deep green of his eyes . . . and then suddenly she heard him speak, as from a long way off . . .

"You have no idea," Parker whispered, "what you're getting yourself into."

The bell rang.

It shattered the hold of his stare, and as Robin gasped and twisted free, she felt Parker's hand slide from her face.

He stepped back and grinned at a gaping Faye.

"Later," he said and was gone.

For several seconds Robin just stood there, staring at the spot where Parker had been standing, then staring down at the crumpled tissue in her hand.

Faye groaned. "I hate you."

"What?" Turning to face her friend, Robin saw the expression of disbelief on Faye's face.

"This is the second day in a row he's talked to you! And you don't even care! Everyone else would *die* for a look from this guy—and *you* don't even *care!* You need a brain transplant, Robin. What is *wrong* with you?"

"He knew your name, didn't he?" Robin muttered. She clamped her books to her chest and started walking.

"You're *right!*" Faye brightened. "He *did* know my name—he said it out loud! Oh, Robin, I just might get that date before Vicki after all!"

"Good luck," Robin said sarcastically, and the two of them ran for class.

It was impossible to concentrate. As Robin stuck out her tongue and ran it gingerly over both lips, searching for cuts, she caught Mrs. Grouse's startled look and slid lower in her seat. She could see people staring at her from the corner of her eye. Embarrassed, she closed her mouth and leaned forward, burying her face in her math book. She couldn't believe she'd made such a total fool of herself out there in the hall. Her body felt hot and then cold, and her chin still tingled from the touch of Parker's hand. *Damn him!* What an ego he had! What an insensitive macho—

"Robin," Mrs. Grouse said, "do you have a problem?"

"No, thank you. I'm okay."

She could still hear Parker's voice in her mind . . . the last thing he'd said to her as he'd left . . . she could still feel the unsettling power of his eyes. Squirming in her chair, Robin looked up and saw Walt giving her a sidelong glance, his eyebrow raised knowingly. *But he couldn't know —he couldn't know what I'm thinking!* Flushing again, Robin lifted her book even higher.

"All right, people." Mrs. Grouse waved a sheaf of papers in the air. "I was very disappointed in these tests. I expected better of you. Robin—"

Robin's heart sank. She lowered her book, barely acknowledging the teacher with a nod.

"Robin, it looks as if you're the only one who bothered to study for this." Mrs. Grouse gave one of her rare smiles. "All you other people—shame on you."

Robin cringed as dark looks shot in her direction.

"Traitor," Walt mumbled.

She shrugged as Faye glared at her, and when class was finally over, she waited in the hall, bracing herself for the lecture she knew would come.

"I hate you even more." Faye scowled, crumpling her test paper and tossing it into a trashcan. "When I think of all that sleep I missed for nothing!"

"Sorry." Robin sighed. "I guess I just have a head for math."

"You have a head for *everything* that anyone could ever get graded on," Faye said glumly. "You're really getting on my nerves."

"Hey, Bailey," a soft voice spoke behind them, "don't you ever get tired of showing off?"

The girls looked up in surprise. Walt was standing in the doorway, that funny little half smile on his face. Robin tried to think of a clever reply, but Faye didn't give her the chance.

"Maybe you and *I* should study together," she said coyly. "Since we're obviously the ones who need . . . practice."

Walt looked straight at her.

"No, thanks."

Even with all the chaos in the hall around

them, Robin felt the sudden, sickening silence. She also saw the angry flush go over Faye's cheeks and the sullen toss of Faye's head as she took a step away.

"Excuse me," Faye said with icily forced sweetness. "I hate to be rude, but I have to go flunk another class now."

"Faye—"

Robin reached for her, but Faye disappeared into the mob of rushing students. After a second of indecision Robin turned solemnly back to Walt.

"You hurt her feelings."

"I'm sorry. What was I supposed to say?"

Robin stared at him.

"That you want to study with her," she said at last, even as Walt was shaking his head.

"But I don't."

The bell sounded, and Robin took a step backward. As a rush of students surged through the hall, someone slammed into her, shoving her up against Walt's chest, and his arm went around her to steady her.

Robin gasped. "Oh, sorry . . . I'm so sorry—"

"I'm not."

Startled, Robin looked up at him. His dark eyes gazed back at her calmly, and a slow smile eased across his lips. Several seconds passed before his arm finally slid from her shoulders.

"Well . . ." Robin glanced back this time before she took a step. "Well . . . I guess I'll see you later."

He nodded. He gave his not-quite sort of smile and walked off in the other direction.

Faye was right—yesterday was a weird day, but today is even weirder. In fact, I can't even imagine anything turning out any weirder than it already is. . . .

Late for class now, Robin turned the corner and headed for the stairs. The hallway was deserted here, and doors were closing up and down the corridor as teachers started their lectures. Picking up speed, she raced down, digging through her notebook for her homework assignment.

She wasn't really watching where she was going.

She didn't even notice the pitiful heap at the bottom of the stairs until she was practically on top of it.

At the last second Robin's head came up, and she gasped in alarm, swerving to avoid a collision.

There was something almost familiar about the body sprawled there on the floor.

Familiar . . . and somehow frightening.

The flowing blond hair . . . the childlike face . . . and the glassy eyes staring up at Robin in horror.

6

My God," Robin whispered. "Claudia . . ."

Robin would have known her anywhere.

She looked just like the portrait of Lillith that Robin had seen hanging at Manorwood last night.

For several horrible seconds Robin could only stare, but then at last she knelt down on the floor and leaned over the prone figure.

"Are you all right?" she burst out. "Are you hurt? Say something—are you—"

"Pushed," the girl mumbled, and as Robin put her arms around her, the girl sagged against Robin's shoulder. "Pushed," she whispered again.

"Can you sit up?" Robin was afraid to move her and looked frantically up and down the hallway for help. "Wait here," she said softly. "I'm going to get the nurse—"

"No!" As if she'd suddenly found some inner reserve of strength, the girl sat up and pushed Robin away. "I don't want the nurse. Really . . . just . . . just leave."

Robin looked at her in surprise. "Come on, it'll be all right. I just don't want you to move in case anything's—"

Robin's voice cut off as she heard footsteps coming leisurely down the stairs, two at a time. She opened her mouth to call for help and saw Parker Swanson's face come into view.

They saw each other at the exact same moment.

Robin's eyes widened and so did his, and in one quick movement he was squatting beside them, tossing his books to the side.

"What happened?"

Robin shook her head at him. "I don't know—I just—"

"Claudia, are you okay?" Parker looked worried, but as he tried to take hold of the girl, she grew even stiffer and pulled out of his reach.

"You know what happened," she murmured. *"You know."*

Robin saw a quick, unreadable expression flicker over Parker's face. He opened his mouth, then shut it again and stood back up.

"I'll try to find the nurse," he said to Robin. "Can you stay with her?"

"Sure."

He disappeared down the hallway, and as

Claudia stared after him, Robin had a moment to study the girl.

If Robin hadn't known about the death of Claudia's mother, she would have sworn that Lillith lay on the floor beside her now. Claudia's face was tiny and oval shaped, her eyes a beautiful shade of violet, and her appearance innocently childlike. Long blond hair streamed over her back and shoulders, and as she lowered her lashes, several tears crept out, though she blinked them fiercely away.

"It's all right," Robin said again. "You're going to be fine."

The girl shook her head but said nothing.

"You're—" Robin broke off, biting her lip. Maybe Claudia didn't know about the cataloging yet—or that Robin had even been to Manorwood. "You're new here, aren't you?"

At last the girl looked her full in the face. Claudia's eyes were so sad, so bewildered, that Robin felt an ache in her own heart.

"I just started here today," Claudia said at last.

"Oh. Well. That explains it."

Robin gave her a reassuring pat, but Claudia remained limp against her.

"That explains it," Robin repeated lamely. "I didn't think you looked familiar."

"Maybe I should get up."

"I'm not sure that's such a good idea—" Robin began, but Claudia's hand clamped tightly onto her arm.

"You must have *seen* her—there on the steps —right before you came down!" The girl's voice rose, and her eyes shot to the top of the empty staircase.

"Who?" Robin asked. "I didn't see anyone. There was just me."

"No," the girl murmured, and again her eyes darted to the landing above. "No, she was there, you see. I have to get up. I have to get away."

Robin tightened her hold around Claudia's shoulders. "But everyone's in class right now— no one's going to come trampling over you. Those stairs are pretty slippery on damp days like this. You're lucky you—"

"I didn't slip. She pushed me."

Robin stared at her. Claudia's delicate brows drew together in a stubborn line, and her eyes lowered to the floor.

"Who?" Robin asked quietly. "Who pushed you?"

For a long moment the girl said nothing.

Then, in a voice barely above a whisper, she said, "It doesn't matter."

Robin felt the fragile body shiver against her. Claudia felt cold and small and helpless.

"But it does matter," Robin tried again. "I can't imagine any of the kids here doing something like that. In the first place they don't even know you. In the second place . . . well . . . they just wouldn't."

"I'd . . . I'd rather not talk about it," Claudia mumbled. Again her eyes blinked, as if fighting back tears, and her face tightened into a mask of soft defiance. "Just leave me alone," she whispered. "Please."

Before Robin could answer, Parker reappeared with the school nurse. Robin stood up and let Miss Danton take over, and after a quick examination it was decided that Claudia had suffered nothing more than bruises and a bad scare.

"Would you like to go home?" Miss Danton offered, but Claudia shook her head adamantly. Apparently Parker had already told the nurse that he and Claudia were related, because now Miss Danton looked questioningly at him. He in turn only looked at the floor.

"Are you sure?" Miss Danton asked again.

"Yes, thank you. I'm fine." Claudia stood slowly and brushed herself off, though Robin could see the girl's hands were still shaking.

"I can take her home if she wants to go," Parker finally said.

Claudia shook her head. Miss Danton nodded.

"Well, why don't you come back with me and lie down for a minute," she said briskly, "just to make sure you're not dizzy. Robin . . . Parker . . . I'll write you two late-notes for class. Thanks for your help."

They watched Miss Danton lead Claudia off to the infirmary, and then Parker turned to Robin with a grin.

"So. Now you've met my crazy grandfather *and* my crazy sister. We're a family full of surprises."

"She wasn't exactly crazy," Robin said, a little stiffly. "She just happened to have fallen down a whole flight of—"

"Yeah, and she told you she'd been pushed, too, didn't she? That it wasn't an accident."

Robin's mouth opened in surprise. "How did you know?"

Parker shook his head and looked smug.

"I told her she'd imagined it," Robin went on quickly. "That no one here would do such a thing. I told her the stairs were slippery and—"

"Her eyes got all big and scared, and you felt sorry for her." Parker leaned over to pick up his books. "Works every time."

"How can you be so cold about it?" Robin burst out angrily.

"Because I know her. After a while you will, too." Parker sighed. "She's just like her mother. And I'm sure my grandfather had a few choice things to say about *her!*"

"Nothing very nice and nothing very concrete," Robin said, bristling. "Everyone seems to be making such a mystery out of the poor woman. All I want to do is get her books in order."

"Her name was Lillith, and she wasn't what I'd call a 'poor woman.'" Parker's tone was sarcastic. "In fact, after she married my father, she was quite rich."

"That's not what I meant, and you know it."

"Oh!" He faked surprise. "I get it! You're talking about the suicide thing! Yes, it's true. Lillith did herself in, but at least she was considerate enough to do it outside. And as for crazy old Claudia—"

"You're disgusting." Robin snatched up her books and glared at him. "And in case you didn't notice just now, Claudia was really scared."

"And you're naive," Parker countered smoothly. "Don't be taken in by what *seems* to be." He looked down at her and grinned. "Except me, of course. Who *seems* to be a wonderful, lovable guy—which I truly *am.*"

Robin turned her back on him and walked away, but he quickly fell into step beside her.

"So we're going to be working in close proximity," he mused. "Hmmm . . . this could turn out to be very interesting. Very enlightening."

"I'm there to work," Robin said sharply. *"If* I take the job at all. I still haven't decided yet."

"Oh, I see." Parker chuckled. "Okay, then, if you *do* decide to take the job—which you *will,* because you find me extremely fascinating and want very much to be close to me—this could turn out to be very educational and professional. Does that suit you better?"

When Robin didn't answer, he reached down and tugged on a strand of her hair.

"You really don't feel comfortable with me, do you?" he teased.

"I just want to get to class," Robin said, avoiding his eyes. "I'm late enough as it is."

"And that really shook you up back there, didn't it? Finding crazy old Claudia like that."

"Well, maybe you think it's funny, but I

don't." Robin bit her lip, still seeing that pathetic heap at the bottom of the stairs. "The poor thing looked so scared . . . so . . ."

"So what?"

Parker stopped, blocking her way. As Robin looked up, startled, his eyes held hers in a merciless stare.

"What were you going to say?" he persisted, his smile slowly fading. "Claudia looked so . . . what?"

"Like she wanted—I don't know—" Robin stammered. "Almost like she wanted me to . . . protect her or something."

Parker's lip curled in a wry smile. He shook his head at her, and the laugh he gave held no humor.

"Forget it, Robin," he said solemnly. "You can't protect Claudia. No one can."

7

Stunned, Robin watched Parker turn and disappear through the door at the end of the hall. She went after him, but by the time she got outside and scanned the grounds behind the school, he was nowhere to be seen. Totally frustrated now, she turned and went back inside.

By noon, reports of the new girl and her accident had already spread, and when Robin sat down in the cafeteria, Faye pounced on her.

"So tell me! How does it feel to be a hero?"

Robin shrugged. "All I did was stay with her until the nurse came. Big deal."

"She's Parker Swanson's sister. That *is* a big deal."

"She was scared and upset. Anybody else would have done the same thing I did."

"I heard Parker was there, too."

"He happened to be coming by."

"Just then?" Faye snorted. "How come he happened by *just then?* Just when *you* were there?"

"He was on his way to class. It was a coincidence. You're making something out of nothing."

"Did he ask you out?"

"Of course he didn't ask me out. He was worried about his sister. Is that all you think about?"

"Whoa—don't bite my head off! I was just asking. I just want to be the first to know, is all. Did you hear the latest?"

Robin shook her head and stared down at her lunch tray.

"Vicki isn't in school today," Faye said triumphantly.

"So what?"

"And she didn't come home last night, either."

This time Robin glanced up. "How come?"

"Nobody knows." Faye moved closer and lowered her head, her voice conspiratorial. "She went out late last night—*sneaked* out! Her folks didn't even know. When she didn't show up this morning, the school called her house, and Mrs. Hastings realized Vicki's bed hadn't been slept in all night."

"So . . . was she with Todd or what?" Robin speculated.

"Okay, here's the thing. She *had* sneaked out to be with Todd—he *admitted* it! But she never showed up at their rendezvous—so he just assumed she changed her mind and wasn't coming!"

Robin's mouth opened in surprise. "Faye—you sound as if you're excited about all this!"

"Well, of course I'm excited about it! You know how Vicki's always talking about doing something really wild! Taking off in the middle of the night—hitchhiking to California—just to see how far she can get before someone catches her!"

"But . . ." Robin looked at her friend in dismay. "What if something's happened to her! What if she's—you know—in trouble or something!"

Faye waved her hand dismissively. "She's not in any trouble! She'll be back! She has to get that condo for us at Thanksgiving. Come on, you know her—she's just being Vicki!"

Robin moved her chair away and bit into her sandwich with a vengeance. She didn't know why she felt so shaken all of a sudden. She was tired of hearing about unsettling things, about Vicki and the condo, about Parker and how wonderful he was. She didn't want to think anymore about that scary painting at Manorwood, and Claudia lying at the foot of the school stairs, and Parker's mysterious comments.

"I heard someone pushed her," Faye said again, and Robin jumped as though she'd been hit.

"What?"

"Claudia." Faye sighed. "Parker's sister! Hello, Robin, anybody home?"

"No one pushed her." Robin shook her head and frowned. "The stairs were empty."

"Well, how do you know? Whoever it was probably ran away by the time you showed up."

"Nobody pushed her. Nobody around here would do something like that."

"Well . . . that's what I heard, anyway."

"Why would anyone push her?" Robin said irritably. "No one even knows her."

Faye made a face. "You don't have to be so touchy."

Robin excused herself and went outside. What little sun there'd been that morning had vanished, and the sky was thickening with clouds. Just like my mood, Robin thought glumly. She wished she'd never gone to Manorwood last night—wished she'd never heard of Claudia and the suicide and Lillith. Suddenly she wanted to race right back and tell Mr. Swanson she didn't want anything to do with any kind of job.

She decided to walk awhile. The weather had kept most of the kids inside, and so she trudged across the yard, glad for the privacy. The grounds behind the school stretched for nearly half a block before finally ending at the gym, with the stadium beyond. As Robin walked slowly around the track that skirted the football field, she was surprised to see a lone figure huddled on the bottom row of bleachers. She was almost past it when something made her study it more closely. She hesitated, then cautiously approached.

"Claudia?" she said softly.

The girl jumped from her seat, whirling with a choked cry.

"It's me," Robin said quickly. "Robin Bailey. I was with you inside—by the stairs. Remember?"

For several seconds she wasn't sure if Claudia recognized her or not. The girl's eyes were huge with suspicion, and her whole body tightened, as if bracing for a dangerous confrontation.

"I just wondered if you were okay," Robin went on. She had a bad feeling that Claudia might turn and run away at any second, and so she stuck out her hand and added, "I guess I really didn't introduce myself."

Claudia watched in silence but made no move to accept the handshake. She simply sat there, and taking this as a positive sign, Robin moved a few steps closer.

"I'm Robin Bailey," she said again, forcing a smile. "You're Parker's sister, right?"

Claudia sighed. "If that's the only reason you want to know me, you're wasting your time."

The surprise on Robin's face was genuine. Claudia must have sensed this, because after a moment she lowered her eyes and shrugged.

"With someone like Parker, you can never be sure who your real friends are."

Robin nodded. "Point taken. Girls haven't been talking about much else since he got here."

Claudia turned her attention to the deserted field.

"I don't live very far from you," Robin said. When Claudia didn't reply, she eased down carefully beside her and laid her books on the bench. "Just about four blocks. If you want, I could come by on my way to the bus. We could walk together."

Claudia's eyes never moved, yet Robin felt herself being scrutinized.

"No, thank you," Claudia said.

Robin hesitated, then tried again.

"Look . . . I know how weird it can be, starting a new school and all—and especially after what happened today, you probably wish you'd never even come. But really, the kids are nice once you get to know them. And I'm glad you're here. I just wanted to say welcome."

There was no response. Robin took a deep breath and plunged on.

"By the way, I was talking to Miss Nelson this morning—she's one of the gym teachers—and it looks like you'll be in my gym class last period. So at least you'll know someone there."

Claudia's shoulders stiffened ever so slightly. After a long moment she turned again, lifting her huge eyes to Robin's face.

"You're the one," she mumbled, and Robin drew back, startled. "Now I know where I've heard your name. You're the one who's going to go through my mother's things."

"Well . . ." Robin didn't know what to say, and from the blank expression on Claudia's face, she couldn't tell exactly how the other girl felt about it. "I answered an ad for the job. I love books—adore books, really—and I was so thrilled that your grandfather hired me. I'll take very good care of everything. And—"

"He's not my grandfather," Claudia interrupted, her voice flat. "Not really. And he hates my mother. He's always hated her."

Robin fell silent. She watched Claudia's nervous fingers twining and untwining themselves in the girl's lap.

"She was a medium, you know," Claudia announced, and she met Robin's surprised gaze head on. "You *didn't* know, did you?"

"No—no, I didn't. Only that she was an artist."

"She had a talent—a *gift,*" Claudia emphasized. "She could talk to the dead. They communicated with her."

A swirl of dead leaves scattered about their feet. Claudia dropped her eyes and watched as the leaves whirled on and on and finally disappeared around the fence.

"What did Parker tell you about me?" she asked softly.

With an effort Robin managed to rouse herself and shrug. "Nothing, really. I didn't even know he had a sister until your grandfather told me."

"I believe that." A sad smile touched Claudia's

face, and she hunched over, burrowing deeper into her coat. "We don't get along, you know. Not Parker, not my grandfather, only Father and me—but he's always out of the country, so I never see him. He married my mother after Parker's mother had her accident, so Parker and I were thrown together against our wills."

Robin looked startled. "What accident?"

"A car accident." Claudia nodded vaguely. "She ran off the road, I think. I've heard she and Parker were very close. So, as you can imagine, there's no great love lost between the two of us."

"He seemed really concerned about you back there today," Robin said generously.

"He'd want you to think that, of course." Claudia's tone was matter-of-fact. "Parker's very big on appearances."

Robin stared at her. Claudia's expression was frozen somewhere between deep unhappiness and a strange sort of resignation.

"Why don't we go inside?" Robin suggested. "You're going to catch pneumonia out here."

Claudia sighed. "Sometimes I think that would be best."

"What are you saying?" Robin chided gently, not knowing quite how to react to that comment. "You're just having a bad day—trust me, I have lots of them. Things will get better."

To her surprise, Claudia fixed her with a pleading look.

"Promise?" she said.

Robin swallowed hard and nodded. "Yes. I promise."

"It's so easy to be optimistic when you're not the one in danger," Claudia said.

Robin had started to walk away, but now she stopped and looked back in alarm.

"Danger? What are you talking about?"

"Nothing." Claudia shook her head and quickly gathered up her books. "Please just forget I said that."

"You can't protect Claudia . . . no one can. . . ."

Parker's words came back with a jolt. *What a stupid thing to say. . . . It doesn't even make any sense.* Annoyed, Robin put one hand to her forehead as if she could rub the memory from her mind.

"How can I forget," Robin said slowly, "when you make it sound so mysterious?"

"I didn't mean to. I don't know why I said it. I wasn't thinking," Claudia babbled. She stood up and stared as Robin reached slowly for her arm.

"Come on," Robin said uneasily. "It's getting really cold out here."

"Cold like the grave." Claudia tilted her chin toward the gray, gray sky. "Cold like death. It's nature's way of preparing us to die, you know."

Robin shuddered. She pulled her jacket tighter and shoved her hands into her pockets, surprised when Claudia began to follow her back toward the building.

For a long while neither girl spoke. Robin wished Claudia would say something more about herself, her house, her family, but to her dismay the other girl began to walk faster, passing Robin up. Robin sighed and concentrated on kicking leaves from her path. She didn't see Claudia come to an abrupt halt ahead of her, and by the time she looked up again, Claudia was reaching out to grab her by the shoulders.

"God, Claudia, you scared me half to—"

"Do you believe in fate?" Claudia interrupted.

She leaned in close, her wide violet eyes only inches from Robin's face. Robin frowned and tried to step back, but for all her delicateness, Claudia's grip was like steel.

"Things happening even when you do everything to *keep* them from happening?" Claudia went on, her voice breathless and urgent. "Things happening just because they're *meant* to, no matter what?"

Robin said nothing. She was still watching Claudia's eyes, the way they kept growing wider and wider with some terrible desperation . . . some awful panic . . . *just like her mother's eyes . . . the eyes in the portrait . . .*

"What is it?" Claudia whispered. Her hands tightened on Robin's shoulders, and she gave her a rough shake, her voice rising in sudden alarm. "What is it, Robin? What do you see?"

"Nothing—I—"

"Don't look at me like that!" Claudia cried. *"Don't look at me!"*

"Claudia—come back!"

But before Robin could move, Claudia turned and raced across the yard, leaving Robin to stare helplessly after.

8

I should be happy about this.

Robin stood outside the gates of Manorwood and looked bleakly through the iron bars. The wind had picked up just since she'd left school, and the trees were groaning, bending low over the fence, reaching out to her with scraggly limbs like claws.

Go on in. Don't be such a coward.

She made herself angry when she acted like this. What did she have to be afraid of, anyway? Old Mr. Swanson had seemed to like her, and she'd already met Claudia. All the preliminaries were out of the way now; all she had to do was get down to work.

So go on in. What's stopping you?

A feeling, Robin decided.

That feeling again of something not quite

right . . . something hanging in the air . . . *like a tragedy about to happen. . . .*

"Stop this! You're being silly," she mumbled to herself. "I need this job, and I'm taking it." The sound of her own voice spurred her to action. She pressed the buzzer by the gate and a moment later found herself walking up the long drive to the house.

"Miss Bailey, no one's home at the moment," Winifred greeted her at the front door. "If you'll just follow me, I'll show you where you'll be working. And if you need anything at all, I'll be glad to help in any way I can."

"Great." Robin smiled. "And please just call me Robin."

Robin liked the woman. In spite of her stiffness, there was something about her that made Robin feel comfortable. Robin followed her down the foyer and through a set of doors into a darkly paneled study. Several lamps had been turned on against the gloomy afternoon, and there was a fire crackling in the fireplace.

"See that bell there?" Winifred jutted her sharp chin in the direction of a mahogany desk where a brass bell rested upon a small brass tray. "If you need me, just ring that and I'll come."

"Thanks," Robin said, shrugging out of her jacket. She tossed it onto a chair, and Winifred immediately picked the jacket up and folded it neatly over one skinny arm.

"You look half frozen," Winifred went on.

"Can I bring you something to drink? Tea? Coffee? Cocoa?"

"Yes, cocoa would be nice." Robin smiled gratefully, and Winifred left her alone.

All of Lillith's books had been transferred into here, Robin noticed at once. There were stacks and stacks of boxes lined along the shelved walls, and more boxes pushed discreetly back behind the overstuffed chairs. Robin wandered over to the desk, where tablets and index cards, pens and pencils were already laid out for her use. A long row of windows framed the cold, gray afternoon.

Well, this is it. Time to get to work.

She walked over, chose a carton, and opened it. The musty smells of damp and age washed over her as she pulled out several books, and then, on second thought, she dragged the whole box over to the desk. She felt like a little kid again, off on some treasure hunt, and as she began digging through the contents, her stomach gave a curious little twist of excitement. *Look at all these books . . . they're so beautiful . . . there're so many of them . . .* She was so intrigued that she hardly even noticed when Winifred brought her cocoa, and it was some time after that before she even thought to check the clock and realized she'd already been there two hours.

This is wonderful. . . . I could spend the rest of my life here doing this.

There were exquisite art books, volume after volume of prints, artists' biographies, and lengthy art histories. Some of the books were positively ancient, and Robin suspected they might also be extremely rare. She handled them carefully, lovingly, afraid that a single breath or misplaced touch might dissolve them to dust. From time to time she came across books of other varied interests hidden among the dusty stacks—human anatomy, science, philosophy, nature—and these, too, she stopped to admire, all the time wondering about the mysterious woman they'd belonged to.

"She could talk to the dead. . . ."

"Lies, lies, lies," Robin mumbled to herself. "All those mediums are fakes. Everyone knows that."

She looked up with a start as a muffled noise brought her back to reality. *A door closing somewhere in the house?* Glancing at the clock, she couldn't believe what she saw—*six-thirty? I've got to get home!*

There were only five books left in the carton. Robin lifted them out and began to scribble information on her tablet, when she heard the noise again.

"Winifred?" she called out. "Is that you?"

No one answered. Robin glanced uneasily around the room.

She hadn't realized how dark it had grown in here. The fire had burned itself down to glowing coals, and darkness had gathered thickly beyond the uncurtained windows. New shadows had crept into the room when she wasn't looking, and now they hovered in corners and crouched among the furniture, giving the room a strange, distorted look.

"Winifred?" Robin called again, but her voice trembled a little. "Are you there?"

I must have imagined it . . . just the wind blowing through cracks . . . just those old noises that old houses make. . . .

She stood up and began putting books back into the box. Then she folded the top down and marked it with a big *X* to show that she'd finished with the contents. She pushed it to one side and was straightening back up when she heard the sound again.

It was closer this time.

Robin didn't know exactly *how* she knew, for the sound was so indistinct—more an impression than an actual noise—and yet a slow chill began crawling up her arms, and her heart beat faster in her chest.

A creaking noise . . . not a door closing . . . something else . . .

She stood there in the shadows and stared. She could see the door open to the hallway beyond, but no light showed past the threshold, and nothing moved. For one panicky instant Robin wondered if she was alone in the house, if Winifred had left her. *Surely someone has to be here—Mr. Swanson—Parker—Claudia—Winifred—where is everyone?* She took a cautious step around the desk, then froze as a voice seemed to float out of nowhere.

"Help . . ."

And she knew she hadn't imagined it this time—the voice so faint and yet so desperate, crying out in the silence of the big, empty house—

"Help me . . ."

"Hello?" Robin called. "Who's there? Where are you?"

"Help . . ."

A woman's voice . . .

And as it spoke this time, it seemed to echo there in the shadows of the hallway . . . hang there, suspended . . . begging Robin to follow. . . .

"Where are you?" Robin called again, and she felt her feet moving her toward the door, even though she didn't want to go, even though she was suddenly so afraid—

The hall lay in pitch blackness.

"Winifred!" Robin pleaded. "Answer me!"

Her words faded to nothing. She took a cautious step out into the passageway and stopped. An icy draft stirred softly around her feet, and she thought she heard another faint, faraway sound of a door closing.

"Winifred . . ."

Every instinct told Robin to run, and yet she knew she couldn't. Suppose Winifred was hurt . . . suppose she'd fallen somewhere . . . Robin couldn't just go off and leave her.

Reaching along the wall, Robin felt for a light switch but found none. She had no idea which way to go, where to look, where to even start. She strained her ears through the darkness, waiting for the call to come again, but there was only silence.

"Winifred!" Robin shouted. "Where are you!"

The air moved restlessly around her . . . like a breath. And when the voice came this time, it seemed to come from everywhere, curling along the shadowed passageway, weaving around Robin like an ice-cold web—

"Help me . . . Claudia . . ."

"It's Robin!" Robin called back. "Please tell me where you are!"

But something was happening now . . . she could see it in the distance, far ahead of her down the hall, and she was so terrified she couldn't move. She could see the strange pale glow shimmering near the floor . . . and she could hear the slow, endless creaking of a door. . . .

"No," Robin whispered.

And yet she began to walk toward it.

She began to walk toward it as one hypnotized, fascinated somehow by that widening crack of light—until she realized that it had been glimmering at her from beneath a door, and now that door was standing wide open, waiting for her to go through. . . .

Robin stood at the threshold and squinted into the gloom.

Shadowy outlines towered high above her . . . indistinct shapes looming up and up, then ending in a hazy burst of light.

Stairs, Robin thought suddenly. *And is that a*

light bulb hanging up there? It didn't seem the sort of staircase to lead to an upper level of rooms in a grand old house like this, she argued with herself. *Then it must be an attic. . . . I bet it's an attic or storeroom or something. . . .*

"Winifred?" she called softly. "Are you up there?"

She thought she heard something move . . . a restless stirring on the floorboards overhead, and her heart leapt into her throat.

Someone is up there—and whoever it is must be hurt and can't answer—I've got to go and see.

Again she searched in vain for a light switch. An image of old Mr. Swanson flashed into her mind, and she imagined him lying up there at the top of those stairs, imagined that he might have been there all afternoon without anyone even knowing. She put her foot on the first step and kept her eyes on the fuzzy light above. And then she began to climb.

The space was narrow and rickety. She could smell dampness and dust, and as she moved cautiously forward, it sounded as if tiny scurrying things moved around her in the walls. The stairs were steep and very long. As Robin finally neared the top, she saw that there was indeed one bare light bulb hanging on a cord from the ceiling, but it was so dim she could hardly make out anything beneath.

"Hello?" Robin called softly, and her voice came back to her mockingly—*Hello . . . hello . . . hello . . .*

She reached the top at last and squinted into the dark.

She didn't know what she expected to see.

Old Mr. Swanson, perhaps, or Winifred, lying there with a broken leg . . .

But certainly not what she *did* see—there in the corner—floating facedown in the claw-footed tub—

The lifeless figure in its long pale dress—hair streaming like wet ribbons . . . and the dark frothy water . . . and the dark trickles down the side . . . and the dark spreading pool on the bathroom floor.

9

It seemed an eternity that she stood there.

Robin opened her mouth to scream, but nothing came out. She stared and she stared and the room throbbed around her in a dreamy fog. And then, as the limp body seemed to move—as it bobbed slowly from side to side—only then was Robin finally able to react—

"No!" a voice shrieked.

It was so close that Robin jumped back against the wall. Above her the light bulb swung in a crazy arc, and she caught just a glimpse of Claudia's stricken face as the girl rushed from the stairs into the room.

"She's *come* for me! I *knew* it! I *knew* it!"

Claudia screamed again and pointed to the corpse as Robin looked on in horror. It was bobbing gently up and down . . . up and down

. . . and the dark pool of water was creeping toward Robin's shoes.

"I told you she'd come for me! She won't leave me alone until I'm dead, too!"

"Claudia!" Robin gasped. "Oh, my God—"

"Now do you see?" Claudia spun toward her, sobbing. *"Now* will you believe me?"

Before Robin could stop her, the girl bolted for the stairs. Robin threw one last horrified look at the thing in the corner and then raced down behind Claudia.

The hallway was empty when Robin got there. As she turned toward the study, the lights flickered once and then went out, plunging the hall into sudden and complete darkness.

"Claudia! Claudia, where are you?"

The police—I've got to call the police—

Frantically Robin groped her way along the corridor, trying to find the study. She knew the passageway was long, but now it seemed interminable, and as her hands slid over door after door, she tried every knob and found them all locked.

"Help! Somebody help! Please!"

She could still see that horrible thing upstairs —could still see it moving—*trying to sit up? Oh, God, what if it really was someone hurt and still alive—and I ran away and I didn't even try to help—*

She wondered if she was losing her mind. She couldn't even think anymore, she was trying so desperately to hurry, her arms out feeling along the walls. Without warning she touched empty air and pitched forward into the dark. She gasped as she fell against something solid, and then she was stumbling, crawling, crashing into furniture as she tried to find her way to the door again.

"Help!" Robin cried. "Oh, Claudia, where are you?"

"What are you doing?" a voice demanded.

Screaming, Robin spun around and saw a shadowy silhouette on the threshold. As it started toward her, she stepped back, groping behind her, and miraculously found the telephone. Robin could only think of one thing now. She jerked up the receiver and started punching 911.

A hand clamped over hers and pulled the phone away.

"What do you think you're doing?" Parker asked again, and as he shone a flashlight into her face, Robin shielded her eyes and tried to draw back from him.

"Let go! I've got to call the police!"

"The police?" Parker sounded bewildered, and his hold tightened around Robin's hand, prying the receiver loose.

"You don't understand!" Robin cried. "There's someone upstairs! Up there in the bathroom—drowned—"

"I told you!" Claudia sobbed, and as Parker's light swiveled to the other side of the room, they could see Claudia framed there in the doorway. "I told you, but you wouldn't—"

Her voice broke off as she took an unsteady

step forward. Robin saw her grab for the door-frame and miss, and in the next instant Claudia crumpled slowly to the ground.

"Claudia!" Robin started toward her, but Parker was quicker. He scooped Claudia up in his arms and laid her down on the couch.

"Is she all right?" Feeling queasy herself, Robin backed away toward the door. At that moment Winifred stepped in from the hallway, holding a candle in front of her, her face ghostly and anxious.

"What is it, Mr. Parker? I thought I heard—oh, my Lord!" The woman crossed herself, and her face seemed to go whiter. "Is she dead? Has Miss Lillith come back for her, just like she said?"

"She fainted," Parker said impatiently. "And don't talk about Lillith in front of Claudia—or me—again. Do you understand?"

Winifred gave a frightened nod and disappeared, but was back again in a second with the water. Claudia had roused a little, and as Parker held the glass to her lips, she coughed and weakly pushed at his arm.

"I'm all right," she mumbled. "Go away."

"But—upstairs—" Robin pointed helplessly toward the foyer, but nobody seemed to be listening. "What are we going to do? We've got to do something!"

Parker stepped away from the couch. Claudia leaned into the cushions, and as Robin heard more footsteps approaching from the corridor,

Mr. Swanson came shuffling in waving another flashlight.

"What's all this?" he barked. "Someone sick? Someone hurt? You'd better tell me—I'll find out soon enough! Winifred? Blast it, turn on a light, will you?"

"I can't turn on the lights, Mr. Swanson—there aren't any lights to turn on!" Winifred babbled. "Tell him, Mr. Parker!"

Robin rushed over and grabbed the old man's sleeve.

"Mr. Swanson—please! You've got to do something!"

"What's that? What are you talking about?"

"Upstairs! Please—hurry!"

"Never mind." Claudia looked at Robin, her voice weak and dull. "It won't do any good. It's not you she wants."

"We've got to call the police!" Robin begged.

"What is she talking about?" Mr. Swanson erupted angrily. "Blast it all, Robin Bailey, I hired you because I wanted someone *sane* in this house for a change!"

"But I *am* being sane," Robin pleaded, "if you'd just listen to me!"

"*You* listen to her!" Mr. Swanson ordered Parker. "Go with her and listen to her and see what the heck she's so upset about!"

"Okay." Parker sighed. "Show me." Even in the dim light Robin could see him exchange looks with his grandfather, who in turn promptly glared at Claudia.

"More of *your* nonsense, I suppose. Can't I get a moment's peace around here? People yelling—lights going out . . . What's the problem, Winifred—did you forget to pay the electric bill? For God's sake, Parker, take another flashlight so you don't fall and kill yourself."

Parker nodded and pulled one from the desk drawer. Then he followed Robin back down the hall.

"There!" Robin pointed to the door at the end of the passageway. It was shut now, but as Parker swung it open, she could see stairs going up into the darkness.

"There's nothing up there," Parker told her. "It used to be a bathroom, but now it's just an old storage—"

"There *is* something!" Robin said fiercely. "I saw it!"

Parker hesitated, as if to speak, then seemed to change his mind. Slowly he started up. Robin followed at a safe distance, her hand over her mouth to hold back a scream. She saw Parker reach the top of the steps, saw him stand for a long moment, saw the slow shrug of his shoulders.

"What are we going to do?" Robin whispered. "We've got to do something!"

"About what?" Parker said.

Robin looked at him blankly. He turned and held out his hand.

"Come up here. I want you to see."

"No, I can't look at it again—I—"

"Come on," Parker said firmly, and he took Robin's hand and pulled her up beside him.

He aimed the flashlight against the opposite wall.

Robin felt her blood go cold.

In the glow of Parker's flashlight Robin could see the old-fashioned bathtub with its claw feet. She could see the straight-backed chair beside it, practically invisible pushed back into the corner, and she could see the dripping mound of wet draperies hanging over the back of the chair and flowing down across the floor.

No body. No spreading pool of blood.

"It—I mean, it can't be! I mean—I saw her!"

Parker groaned. "Saw who?"

"A woman!" Robin turned frightened eyes to Parker's narrowed ones. "I'm not lying—you've got to believe me! She was lying there in the tub and there was all this blood! She had a white dress and long hair—like—like the woman in the painting!"

"A white dress," Parker repeated.

"Yes!"

"About the length of those curtains?"

"Well . . . but it wasn't curtains! I . . . at least, I don't think . . ." Robin's voice trailed off in confusion.

"Was Claudia here with you?" Parker asked.

"Well, yes, I mean not at first—well, yes, she might have been at first—she was behind me—"

"That's what I thought," he said, and Robin stared at him.

"What's that supposed to mean?"

"Nothing," he said. "Come on. Let's go back down."

Robin was dumbfounded. As she followed Parker back to the study, her mind raced in a hundred different directions. They reached the study, and Mr. Swanson looked questioningly at Parker. Parker shook his head, and the old man's face darkened.

"All this commotion!" he sniffed. "Can't an old man take a simple nap anymore? Idiots! I'm surrounded by a bunch of total idiots!"

"Something was up there!" Robin insisted, but Parker turned to Winifred.

"What's that stuff hanging up there in the storage room?" he asked her.

"Storage room?" For a moment the maid's face looked blank, but then she began to nod. "Why, drapes, Mr. Parker. They needed a proper washing, and they wouldn't fit in the machine. So I thought I'd just use that old tub up there—it did nicely."

"See?" There was no mistaking the smugness in Parker's tone, and Robin felt a surge of anger go through her.

"I know what I saw!" she burst out at him.

"Oh, come on, it was an honest mistake." Parker laughed. "And in the bad light—you were nervous—"

"She's come back." Claudia sat up straighter on the couch and stared at them.

The room grew uncomfortably still. Robin saw

Winifred put one hand to her heart. Old Mr. Swanson slammed his fist down on the desk, and everyone jumped.

"Balderdash, I tell you! It's all balderdash! If you keep this up, Claudia, I swear on your mother's grave, I'm going to have you locked up!"

"It wouldn't do any good," Claudia replied calmly. "She'll find me there just like she found me here. She can go anywhere she pleases. She can follow me anyplace I go. I can't hide from her. I can never hide from her. She'll have me when she wants me. It's inevitable."

Even in the shadowy room Robin could see the old man's eyes fairly shooting sparks. The tension in the air was so thick, the room seemed ready to explode.

"Don't you believe me?" Claudia begged. She looked at Robin and her voice tightened. "Don't you believe *her?*"

"I saw something," Robin said.

Everyone stared at her.

"That's why I went up there in the first place," she explained. "I heard someone calling for help. I thought it was Winifred, that maybe she was hurt."

"That wasn't me," Winifred said nervously, "and I certainly wasn't hurt."

"She said Claudia's name."

Claudia went pale. "Me," she whispered. "I told you."

"I *did* call out to Claudia," Winifred said

cautiously, as though afraid she'd be reprimanded for it. "I thought I heard a door slam and that it might be her coming home. I called out to her, but I don't think you could have heard me in the study." She glanced at Robin, then quickly away.

Silence fell again.

"It moved," Robin insisted. "I saw it—it moved in the bathtub like it was trying to get up!"

"Maybe it was waiting for you to hand it a towel," Parker deadpanned.

"It's not funny!" Robin said furiously.

"I didn't say it was! All I said was—"

"I have to go," Robin said stiffly. "I've got to get home."

"If you know what's good for you, you'll never come back," Claudia said.

Everyone looked at her. No one even seemed to be aware Robin was there. At last Parker glanced over, almost as an afterthought.

"Did you drive?" he asked.

Robin shook her head. "No. Walked."

"Then you shouldn't go alone. I'll take you."

"I don't want you to take me. I'd rather walk."

"I'll *take* you," he said and gave a sweeping bow.

Robin clamped her mouth shut. She jumped as Winifred tapped her on the shoulder and magically produced her jacket.

"Thanks," Robin whispered.

The maid nodded and vanished into the shadows down the hall. For a long moment Mr. Swanson glared at Claudia, until finally the girl stood up, held her head high, and walked deliberately past him out of the room.

"Come on," Parker said, and before Robin could even say good night to Mr. Swanson, Parker took her arm and guided her swiftly down the hall and out the front door.

The night was bitingly cold. As Robin zipped up her jacket, the porch light popped on without warning, and she jumped back with a cry.

"It's you, isn't it?" Parker teased. "You have some kind of aura around you. You make lights go off and on and spirits walk."

"If I had powers like that, I'd make you disappear," Robin retorted.

He chuckled and hopped lightly down onto the driveway. She watched as he tried his car door, but when it wouldn't open, he leaned over and peered into the window, then turned back to her, swearing.

"Some evil spirit locked my keys in. Do you care if we walk?"

"I can go alone, I don't need you to—" Robin started, but Parker grabbed her elbow and steered her down the drive.

"I just live over on—"

"I know where you live," Parker said, grinning.

Robin stared at him in confusion. She felt overwhelmed by everything that had happened, and as he ushered her quickly away from

Manorwood and on through the neighboring streets, he seemed almost in a jovial mood.

"Wait," she said at last, stopping on the sidewalk. "I've got to talk about what just happened back there."

"You mean my keys? It's very simple, really. See—you just leave them in the ignition, push the lock on the door, and—"

"Will you be serious—I'm really upset about this!" Robin broke out of his grasp and whirled to face him. "I don't understand what's happening!"

For a long moment Parker stared at her. When he finally answered, his voice was hard.

"Claudia's paranoia is what's happening." Abruptly he turned and started walking again, but he did slow down enough to let Robin catch up.

"Claudia's paranoia? I don't know—"

"She's always seeing things. Predicting things. Particularly her own death—it's a personal favorite of hers."

"But *I* saw something, too! Doesn't that count for anything?"

"Saw something? Or *thought* you saw something? Look, Robin, I don't know what Claudia's told you, but she's a master at getting sympathy. And I've seen you in class long enough to know you're always rooting for the underdog. You don't have to corroborate her story just because you feel sorry for her. She knows exactly what she's doing."

"Parker—"

"She's not what you'd call stable." Parker tapped the side of his head. "Right? She's the one who found her mother—slit wrists and all. If you ask me, Claudia hated Lillith all those years, and if she's trying to get rid of some deep childhood guilt by making up weird nightmares about her mother coming after her, that's *her* problem, not yours."

"I need to sit down," Robin said. She lowered herself to the curb and put her head down on her knees.

"Sorry." Parker sat beside her and stared off down the street. After a moment he put his arm around her shoulder and gave her a shake. "Come on, don't take this thing so seriously. So you thought some curtains were drowning in the bathtub—so what? It could happen to anyone!"

"You're really heartless, you know that?" Robin whispered, but in spite of herself she smiled.

"Thanks," Parker said. "You're too kind."

"But"—Robin drew a shaky breath—"I really thought it was a woman. I really thought it was . . ."

"Lillith?" Parker asked gently, and she nodded.

"Lillith . . . or Claudia . . . I don't know what I thought." Robin sighed. "It was just so awful."

"You can't save Claudia, so forget it. For the longest time I tried to get close to her after Dad married Lillith—Claudia didn't want anything to do with me. So finally I stopped trying. She's a strange kid. She fantasizes . . . makes things up. Sees things that aren't there."

"Do you think she's . . . you know . . . dangerous?"

"To herself? Yeah, I think she could be suicidal, and I also think it wouldn't take too much to push her right over the edge. I just give her space and go my own way and let her go hers. Then everyone's happy."

Again Robin nodded. Things still weren't any clearer, but she at least felt calmer.

"Okay?" Parker nudged her.

"I guess so."

"Then come on. I better get you home. Your folks will be worried about you."

"No, my mom never gets home till late."

"She doesn't?" he asked casually.

"No. She works and then she goes to school at night. She and my dad are divorced, and he lives with his new wife in Rome."

"No siblings to fight with?"

"My older brother, Brad. But he's away at college."

"So you're alone a lot."

Robin glanced at him. A little shiver of apprehension went up her spine.

"Yes," she said and wondered why she suddenly wished she hadn't said anything at all.

Parker helped her up and they kept walking, neither of them speaking again till they reached her house. He waited while she unlocked the door, and then he took a step back, the old cocky grin back on his face.

"If you need protection, just call me," he teased.

"Protection from what?"

He shrugged. "You never know."

"I'll keep that in mind." She waved and locked the door behind her.

She was exhausted.

She went up to her room and ran a hot bath. She couldn't get the strange evening out of her mind. She kept seeing the stairs looming above her and that lifeless form floating in the bathtub and that dark spreading pool across the floor . . .

"She's the one who found her mother—slit wrists and all. . . ."

"I don't want to think about it," Robin told herself fiercely. She decided to do some of her homework while she soaked in the tub, so she picked up her history book and eased herself down beneath the suds.

"Oh, no."

It only took a glance to realize the book wasn't hers. Robin stared at it in dismay, remembering how she'd stopped to talk to Claudia at lunchtime and how their books had been lying side by side on the bleachers. *I must have accidentally picked up the wrong one.*

As Robin prepared to put the book aside, she saw a plain white envelope fall out and land in the water. Quickly she scooped it up, then pulled out the small piece of paper inside to dry it on her towel. She didn't mean to read the message, but when she saw the strange writing, she knew something was wrong.

It was wild writing, manic writing, and the color of it wasn't like any ink Robin had ever seen before.

It had dried to an ugly reddish brown, swashed in thick uneven streaks, and there were drops splattered messily all over the paper and in between the letters.

Blood? Dried blood?

Robin felt as if she was going to be sick.

And yet still she had to read the message . . . again . . . and yet again . . .

CLAUDIA, I'M COMING FOR YOU.

And the message was signed, MOTHER.

10

Mother," Robin repeated dully.

She didn't see the bathroom door begin to open . . .

Or the hand slide around one corner of the door . . .

"Mother," she said, louder this time.

"Robin?" the voice answered, and Robin shrieked as her own mother stuck her head into the room.

"Goodness, Robin, I thought you heard me come in! I didn't mean to scare you. How'd the new job go today?"

"New job?" Robin stared, her mind racing. "It went . . . great. I love it. It's going to be . . . great."

"Great." Mom gave her a puzzled look. "Class was called off tonight, so I went by the store.

Could you give me a hand with the groceries—the trunk's full of them."

"Yeah, just let me throw on some clothes."

"Please do," Mom teased and closed the door behind her.

Robin shut her eyes and took a deep breath. Then she stared down at the bathwater. The note was floating facedown among the suds where she'd dropped it, and when she lifted it up again, the paper was curled and soggy and . . . blank.

Someone's playing a joke on Claudia—a cruel, vicious joke. What else could it be? But I've got to tell her about this note . . . don't I? How can I tell her? Maybe I shouldn't tell her. It'll just upset her. But maybe she's already seen it—maybe someone already put it there and she already read it and that's why she acted so strange when we talked on the bleachers. . . .

Robin dressed quickly and went downstairs. She didn't want to think about her job anymore —not Manorwood, not Claudia, not Parker, not anything. It was so seldom that Mom got home early, and she wanted to make the most of it. They made pizza and popped popcorn and watched videos that Mom had rented at the grocery store. But through it all, Robin's mind was somewhere else, no matter how hard she tried to concentrate. She kept seeing Claudia's pale, frightened face . . . *so much like the face in the portrait* . . .

It was a relief to finally crawl into bed. Robin pulled the blankets up to her chin and burrowed deep beneath their warmth. *Maybe Parker's right . . . maybe Claudia really is crazy . . . imagines crazy things . . .*

But you saw that thing in the bathtub. And it didn't look like curtains when you saw it the first time.

So maybe I'm crazy, too. Maybe it's contagious.

Robin groaned and pulled the covers over her head. The whole thing was ridiculous—too fantastic to even worry about, much less believe. She wouldn't think about it anymore. Winifred had simply been calling Claudia, and Robin had followed the sound accidentally to the storage room, and both she and Claudia had seen the curtains floating there in the dim light . . . *and then they hopped out of the tub by themselves and hung themselves over the chair to dry.*

You don't believe any of it, Robin told herself angrily. *So stop trying to convince yourself that it all makes sense.*

She wasn't ready for the alarm to go off at seven; she felt as if she'd just lain down and closed her eyes. She got dressed in a half stupor and grabbed some cookies to munch on the way to school, but when she opened the door to go outside, she nearly fell over a lump huddled on her doorstep.

"Claudia!" Robin exclaimed. "What are you doing here?"

Claudia looked terrible. Her eyes were smudged with black hollows, and Robin could tell the girl hadn't slept all night, either.

In spite of her disheveled appearance, Claudia managed a wan smile.

"Waiting for you," she said calmly.

Robin hesitated, then sat down beside her on the porch.

"Are you okay?"

Claudia stared at her a moment, then slowly shook her head. The violet eyes filled with tears.

"Not really."

On an impulse Robin reached out and put her arm around the other girl's shoulders, giving her a quick squeeze.

"Me, neither. But oatmeal cookies always give problems a clearer perspective, don't you think?"

Claudia looked startled as Robin held out a cookie. Then, smiling almost shyly, she accepted it and took a cautious bite.

"Specialty of the house." Robin chuckled. "My mom doesn't do much cooking, but this I insist upon. Of course, it helps having a brother away at college who constantly needs care packages sent with his favorite food in them."

Claudia considered this a minute. "You really love your brother, don't you?"

"Yeah." Robin smiled, thinking of him. "I miss him a lot. We're buddies."

"Must be nice."

"Oh." Robin bit off a raisin and thought a minute. "You know . . . Parker really doesn't seem so bad."

"Not to you. He thinks you're wonderful."

"He does?" Robin asked, surprised, then

quickly tried to act indifferent. "I didn't know that."

"I haven't heard him talk about any other girls," Claudia said. "That must mean something."

Robin didn't answer. She chewed a long time.

"Claudia," she ventured at last. "I got your book by mistake yesterday. And . . . I found something in it. By accident."

Claudia's look was instantly suspicious. Robin took a deep breath and went on.

"Here." She pulled the note from her purse. It was stiff and curled, and as she handed it over, Claudia's look was equally as blank.

"There's nothing on it."

"I know. I dropped it in the bathtub."

Claudia stared at her.

"The thing is," Robin went on uncomfortably, "the note was . . . upsetting. Claudia—I think someone is trying to play a joke on you. A really mean joke. Do you know anyone who would want to upset you like that?"

"What did it say?"

"It said"—Robin took another deep breath— "well, someone wanted you to think it was from your mother."

"Wanted me to think?" A deep shudder went through Claudia's body. "If it said it was from her . . . then it was from her." She lowered her head into her hands and hunched her shoulders forward.

"Come on, Claudia, you don't really believe

your mother is sending you notes from the dead, do you? It just doesn't happen and—"

"You don't even know my mother!" the girl said sharply. "You don't know what she was like! She had powers! If they were that strong when she was alive, then how much stronger must they be now from the other side! Don't you see—I don't have a chance. She *wants* me with her, and she'll do anything to get me!"

"But why?" Robin insisted. "Why would your mother want to hurt you?"

"Because I didn't help her!" Claudia's voice rose and her body went rigid. "Because she begged me to help her and I didn't help! I just . . . let her die."

She buried her face in her hands and began to cry softly. Robin watched her for a moment, then put a cautious hand on her shoulder.

"Claudia, you didn't even know! There wasn't anything you could do. It wasn't your fault. And I don't believe for a minute that your mother wants to hurt you. But I do believe that someone wants you to *think* she does."

The crying stopped. "Who then?" Claudia whispered.

Robin shook her head. "Who do *you* think?"

Claudia's small hands wiped tiredly at her tear-stained cheeks.

"Well . . . Parker of course. He hates me. And his grandfather hates me. He never liked me *or* my mother. Father is out of the country, but I've never doubted his love for me." At this she smiled a bit, but then it faded almost instantly. "So . . . you're saying . . . you think someone is deliberately trying to . . . drive me crazy?"

Robin sat back and sighed. "Whew. That's pretty strong. Sitting here talking about personal stuff like this when I don't even really know you well enough to . . ." She saw Claudia lower her eyes sadly, and she rushed on. "It is *possible,* isn't it?"

"But . . . why?"

"That's what I was hoping you could tell me."

"Hate? Is that reason enough? Jealousy?"

"How so?"

"Father usually pays more attention to me than to Parker when he's home. The two of them have never gotten along very well—Parker was always closer to his mother. But his grandfather has *always* favored Parker. So really, if you look at it that way, that makes Parker and me sort of equal."

"Some other reason?"

"Well . . . money?"

Robin looked interested. "What about the money?"

"An inheritance." Claudia seemed uncomfortable. She hesitated and plucked nervously at her skirt. "What money that should have gone to my mother will go to me on my eighteenth birthday."

"And does Parker stand to inherit anything?"

"Yes. His mother's share, of course. But . . ."

Claudia fell silent. The quiet dragged on for so long that Robin finally reached out and shook the girl gently.

"But what?" she urged.

Claudia's look was half reluctant, half sad. "Father wants to divide up the rest of the money —his and grandfather's shares—evenly between Parker and me. But Grandfather refuses. He wants Parker to have it all. And he's the one who still controls the money."

"And how does Parker feel about it?"

"I don't know. But sometimes I hear them talking—arguing, really—Father and him behind closed doors. I can't hear what they're saying. And if I come into the room, they get quiet. And then Parker usually looks upset and leaves."

"So what you're saying is . . ."

"What I'm saying is, that if *I* wasn't here, then Parker would get it all."

"All of it? Like . . . a huge amount?"

"The whole family fortune," Claudia said wryly. "It can't get much bigger than that."

"Wow." Robin hugged her knees to her chest and thought a moment. It was Claudia's voice that finally broke into her reverie.

"If you're thinking what I *think* you're thinking, then don't," Claudia said firmly. "Parker has nothing to do with this at all. It's my *mother* who's after me, not Parker."

Robin's first instinct was to ask Claudia how she could be so sure, but instead she kept quiet.

"Just the money we inherit from our mothers is more than Parker or I could ever spend in a lifetime," Claudia went on. "And since Grandfather's opinion is really the only one that counts in this family, Parker has no reason to be jealous—or afraid—of me."

Robin shrugged. "Money does strange things to people."

"I don't believe it," Claudia said tightly. "Parker and I may not get along most of the time, but I can't see him trying to hurt me or drive me insane just for some extra money he'll probably get anyway. No, I don't believe that."

"He showed up right after you fell at school yesterday," Robin ventured cautiously. "He could have been in the house last night setting up that scene in the attic."

"No."

"And after the lights went out, he could have rearranged the bathroom—"

"No!"

Claudia clamped her hands over her ears, and Robin drew a deep breath.

"I'm sorry, Claudia. I should never have brought it up."

Claudia got to her feet, clearly flustered.

"Let's go. We can talk on the way."

They started off down the street, neither of them speaking. The morning was thick with fog, and houses crouched far back on the lawns like living, watchful things. Robin suppressed a shudder as the wind moaned through the dead trees. The girls reached the corner and started across to the other side.

Robin saw the car slipping out of the fog, but she didn't pay too much attention.

She saw it cruise noiselessly to the corner two blocks away and idle there, alone. She saw it start to move again, and as it began to pick up speed, she had one fleeting thought that it was driving too fast. But when it squealed around the corner, she suddenly realized it was heading the wrong direction down a one-way street.

"Claudia," she called, "look out for that car over there."

But Claudia didn't seem to hear.

She had stopped and was staring, her eyes wide, her mouth locked in a silent scream.

"Claudia!" Robin shouted. "Get out of the way!"

But Claudia stood frozen, like a small, pale statue in the middle of the street.

"Claudia!"

Robin lunged toward the girl and in her panic caught just a glimpse of the driver as the black car bore down relentlessly on top of them.

What she saw paralyzed her, every bit as stonelike as Claudia.

The figure behind the wheel wasn't human.

It had no face.

It stared straight ahead out of black hollow eye sockets, and what little flesh remained on its gleaming skull hung there in long bloody strips.

Robin screamed in horror.

She saw Claudia spread her arms wide . . . step into the path of the car . . . and smile.

11

Claudia!" Robin shrieked. "Look out!"

At last she was able to move again. She dived for the other girl, but out of nowhere a blur flew past her, slamming into Claudia as the black car gunned its engine and peeled off down the street. Robin fell to her knees beside the sprawled, tangled bodies on the curb and looked down into Walt's angry face.

"Walt—my God—"

"Wait here," Walt ordered. He jumped to his feet and raced to the middle of the street, but the car had long since disappeared. He ran back again to the curb and knelt down beside Robin, who was trying to roll Claudia over onto her back.

"Did I hurt her?" Walt asked anxiously. "Is she breathing?"

"Robin?" Claudia looked dazed. "What happened?"

"Did you get a look at the license number?" Walt asked, but Robin shook her head.

"No—it happened so fast. But I saw the driver—"

"Mother's car." Claudia closed her eyes and didn't see the other two staring at her.

"What did you say?" Robin whispered.

"My . . . mother drove a car like that. It was my mother's car."

"Your mother's car? That must have been some fight you two had this morning," Walt mumbled, more to himself than to Claudia.

"What do you mean, your mother's car?" Robin demanded.

"I . . . I mean . . . she drove a black car. . . ."

"Come on, there are millions of black cars around," Walt said offhandedly, throwing a mildly curious glance in Robin's direction. "Someone was just late for work and they weren't watching where they were going."

"You don't understand," Robin said impatiently, nudging him aside. "Claudia's mother happens to be dead." She ignored the stare he fixed upon her, and she leaned in closer to Claudia. "Do you still have your mother's car?"

"No. Grandfather sold it after she died."

"Is there something about all this I should know?" Walt asked calmly.

"We need to report this," Robin said, rocking back on her heels, putting her hands on her hips. "Shouldn't we? Shouldn't we report this to the police?"

Walt sighed and stood back up. "I'd sure like to read *this* report."

Robin gazed up at him. "I'm serious."

"I can see that. So what exactly are we reporting? The part about the car or the part about Claudia's mother? Or the part about—"

"This, of course," Robin broke in. "This car trying to run Claudia down."

"We can't prove the car was trying to run Claudia down. The driver might just have been having a bad day."

Not this driver, Robin thought grimly, but instead argued, "You saw it! You saved her life!"

"We can't *prove* anything," Walt said again patiently, and Robin bit her lip in frustration.

Claudia raised tearful eyes, and when she spoke, her voice was shaking.

"Did you see who was driving?"

Robin stared at her. "No," she said, turning away. "It happened too fast."

She ducked her head and saw Walt throw her a curious glance. Together they helped Claudia to her feet and brushed her off.

"Are you sure you're okay?" Robin worried, but Claudia managed a feeble smile.

"I think so. What about you? And . . . you?" She glanced almost shyly at Walt, and he gave an absentminded nod.

"My adrenaline's in fine working order for the day, thanks very much."

"What were you doing here anyway?" Robin wanted to know. "Not that I'm complaining or anything. . . ."

"I just stopped by Jim's house to see if there was any news about Vicki," he said, and Robin frowned.

"And is there?"

Walt shook his head. "Not a word. Not even a clue. It's like she just walked off the face of the earth."

Robin shuddered and handed Claudia her books.

"Who's Vicki?" Claudia asked.

"A girl in our class," Walt filled her in. "Her brother Jim's on the debate team with me. Apparently she sneaked out the other night and never came home. Nobody knows where she is."

"Maybe she got run down by a speeding car," Claudia murmured.

Robin glanced at Walt. "Faye thinks she ran away."

"Faye just *wishes* Vicki ran away so she can sink her claws into Parker Swanson," Walt said amicably. "Anyway, her family's pretty upset. The police were there when I left. They're probably going to question a bunch of us at school today."

"That really gives me the creeps." Robin shivered. "Let's go."

The three walked along in silence until Robin let out a sigh.

"Well, what are we going to do about this? I keep thinking we need to tell the police."

"Tell them what?" Walt asked. "Obviously more than you've told me."

"That we nearly got killed, that's what."

"We don't have a make or a license plate, much less a description of the driver," Walt said, and Robin suppressed another shiver.

"And who would believe us anyway, right?" Robin mumbled. "They never believe kids. They sure won't believe us."

Claudia's eyes were huge and sad. "You're right, of course." She glanced at Walt and added softly, "Thank you for what you did back there. I'm Claudia."

"Walt." He gave her that halfway smile of his, and Robin broke in quickly.

"Sorry, that was rude of me. I should have introduced you."

"It seems to me you have a lot on your mind." Walt's glance was meaningful, but then he turned back to Claudia. "Parker's sister, right?"

Claudia nodded but said nothing.

"Sorry. I'm not one to go by labels." Walt smiled lazily and shifted his books to his other arm. "I don't know Parker that well. He's in my drama class. Pretty good, too."

"He loves to act," Claudia said dryly. "It's one of the things he's best at."

"Yeah?" Walt sounded interested.

"He always had leads in the school plays where he used to live," Claudia said. "My mother—"

She broke off, caught her breath, and tried again. "My mother always said he was very good. Very talented. She said he had a way of taking on the personalities of the people he played . . . so that he was totally believable."

Robin frowned. She stared down at her shoes scuffing along the pavement, and when she glanced up again, Walt was staring at her with his eyebrows raised. She flushed and looked away, relieved when they finally got to school. After homeroom, on her way into math class, Walt suddenly appeared and touched her on the elbow.

"I want to talk to you," he said.

"About what?"

"I don't know. But I think *you* do," he said, and Robin purposely kept her eyes averted from him all during class.

She managed to avoid Walt by ducking into the bathroom when the bell rang, and the rest of the day she was so busy with her usual routine, she practically forgot about what had happened that morning. Gossip of the day centered on Vicki Hastings and her strange disappearance— everyone had a theory about what had happened, from demented stalkers to ransom money, but the general consensus seemed to be that Vicki had finally hitchhiked off to California where she'd always threatened to go. Robin felt bad for Jim and his family but didn't have much time to dwell on it—she had enough things on her own mind.

She hadn't had a chance to really talk to Faye. There'd only been time for quick chatter between classes, and when Robin searched for her at lunch, Faye had been eating with Zak. *She has no idea how crazy my life is right now,* Robin thought glumly as she walked down the hall to her locker—*and I'm not sure I can even begin to explain it.* She barely glanced at the bulletin board as she passed it, but then, as something caught her eye, she stopped and backed up.

The cluttered confusion of junk still covered the wall, but as Robin's gaze fell on the class picnic photos, she noticed that several were missing.

Vicki's.

And mine.

Robin glanced around the hallway and rubbed a sudden chill from her arms. *It doesn't mean anything,* she told herself firmly. *Someone probably took Vicki's down because of her disappearing, got rid of it so it doesn't upset people to see her smiling there on the bulletin board. And mine could have fallen or maybe gotten trashed— nobody would want a picture of me.*

She wondered if anyone had even noticed it besides her. So much more stuff had been added to the board, the photos were practically hidden now anyway. *Maybe Jim took Vicki's picture down. To give to the police or something.*

She opened her locker and traded her books for her gym suit. She was so deep in thought that at first she didn't even notice Claudia standing there waiting for her.

"Claudia!" Robin exclaimed. "Is anything wrong?"

The girl looked exhausted. Her face seemed even paler than it had that morning, and her eyes had a haunted, bruised look that spoke silently of tension and fear. As Robin stared in concern, Claudia managed a brave smile.

"I . . . I was just wondering . . . if you were going—you know—to the house today after school?"

She doesn't want to go home alone, Robin thought grimly. *And I don't blame her.*

"I plan to," Robin said. "At least for a little while."

"I thought maybe you'd have a date," Claudia said. The two of them headed for the outside door and started across the yard toward the gym.

"I never have a date." Robin sighed. "But *you* certainly shouldn't have any trouble."

"Parker tells me I'm so strange that no one will ever ask me out."

"Oh, what does Parker know?" Robin threw back at her and was glad to see Claudia smile again. "I'll introduce you to some of the guys, if you want. In fact, I'll introduce you to everyone." She gave Claudia a scolding look. "You were pretty antisocial yesterday."

Claudia flushed. "I know I was. I just wasn't ready to meet people."

"Well, I'm telling you, today's volleyball day, and I'm picking you for my team."

"I'm not very good," Claudia warned her, but Robin laughed.

"That's a relief. I thought I was the only one."

The class went by quickly. To Robin's surprise, her team won for a change, and afterward she spent half an hour ushering Claudia around from one friend to another. The locker room had nearly emptied by the time introductions were over, and as the two girls began to undress, Robin gave Claudia a victory sign.

"You did great. See? No one bit you."

"No," Claudia agreed, smiling tiredly. "They all just want me to get them a date with Parker."

"Let them get their own dates." Robin tossed Claudia's towel at her and led the way into the showers. "Come on, I'll race you. I can't stand smelling like dirty socks."

"What are all these signs?"

"Oh," Robin grunted. "Out of order again. You'll get used to that here, Claudia. Only a few of these showers almost ever work at one time. Let's try these two at the end."

The hot water felt good and soothing, and as Robin let it flow through her hair, she concentrated on emptying out her mind as well—all the troubled thoughts sloughing off and swirling down the drain. Claudia was actually beginning to act a little bit normal; at least she'd made an effort to talk to the girls just now, and she seemed to want Robin's company. *It'll just take time,* Robin thought to herself, *and why shouldn't it, after all Claudia's been through. . . .*

She raised her voice a little so it would carry to the stall next to hers.

"You okay over there?"

For a moment there was silence. Frowning, Robin started to call again, when Claudia's voice answered.

"How long does it take this water to get hot?"

"I don't know. Not too long."

"It's kind of creepy in here, isn't it?"

"No creepier than any other afternoon, except it's Friday and it empties out faster. Don't worry —Miss Nelson's office is just down the hall," Robin reassured her. "And so is Coach Marvin's. They never leave till everyone's out."

She closed her eyes and tilted her head back beneath the running water.

"Robin?" Claudia called softly.

"What?"

"Something's . . . weird."

"Weird how?"

"Like . . ." Claudia's voice rose. "Like . . . someone's watching me."

Robin's eyes flew open. Instinctively she turned around, her eyes quickly scanning the area outside the shower stalls.

"You've been seeing too many scary movies," she said, trying to laugh it off. "No one could watch us—there's no place for anyone to hide."

Claudia didn't answer. Robin peeked out again and suppressed a shiver. The water was steaming hot, yet she suddenly felt chilled.

"Did you hear that?" Claudia asked nervously.

Robin hesitated, her fingers tangled in her hair. A slow rash of goose bumps crawled over her body.

"What?" she whispered.

And yet for just a second she'd thought . . .

No, that's silly. Now I'm imagining things.

"A voice." Claudia's answer was muffled, and Robin had to strain to hear. "Someone talking."

"Miss Nelson?" Robin shouted. "Is that you?"

Her words echoed back to her, hollow and distorted. There was only the dull roar of the water spraying and the sudden thud as her soap fell onto the tiles. Robin nearly jumped out of her skin.

"Miss Nelson!" Robin shouted louder this time. "Who's there?"

And she could *swear* she'd heard a voice just then . . . the faintest sound of someone calling. . . .

"I bet it's some of the guys," she said with forced confidence. "I bet they're out in the hall trying to scare us."

"Do you think so?" Claudia peeked cautiously around the corner of the stall, but she didn't look convinced. "Robin, maybe we should get out of here."

"I'm not going to let a bunch of stupid guys run

us off," Robin said with more courage than she felt. "Are you finished?"

"No." Claudia shook her head. "The water's still cold."

"Try another one, then." Squinting through her wet hair, Robin peered down the line of shower stalls. "Down there—near the other end."

Claudia wrapped up in a towel and tiptoed quickly down the hall. Then suddenly she stopped and cast Robin an anxious glance back over her shoulder.

"What is it?" Robin asked.

"That sign." Claudia's voice trembled as she pointed straight ahead of her.

"What sign?"

"That out-of-order sign." Claudia hesitated, then added slowly, "Wasn't it on that other shower stall when we got here?"

For a moment Robin could only stare at her, bewildered.

"The sign," Claudia said again nervously. "Wasn't it on that *last* stall?"

Robin looked from Claudia to the sign and back again.

"Claudia, there are half a dozen out-of-order signs in here—how could you possibly tell which one was hanging on which shower stall when we walked in? And how could it possibly have moved?" She paused, watching fear and suspicion struggle over Claudia's features. "And why," Robin added more kindly, "would you even *think* it moved?"

"I don't know," Claudia mumbled, putting one hand to her forehead. "I just . . . thought I heard something again."

"When?"

The other girl dropped her eyes. "It doesn't matter. Maybe I just—"

"It does matter," Robin said. "Claudia?"

Shaking her head, Claudia disappeared into the end stall. Robin waited several seconds, then ducked uneasily back into her own shower, burying herself once more beneath the muffling rush of hot water.

She squeezed out her washcloth and reached up to rinse her hair.

And this time she knew she hadn't imagined it.

"Help . . ."

It seemed to be laughing now. A strange mocking sort of laugh. Floating out of nowhere, yet very close, so very dangerously close—

"Help me . . ."

"Robin!" Claudia screamed.

But Robin was already running.

"Claudia!" she shouted. "Claudia, are you all right?"

"Oh, Robin—*what's happening!*"

Robin swung around the corner of Claudia's shower stall.

And froze.

And pressed one hand to her mouth to keep from being sick.

At first she didn't see Claudia.

There was only the slimy red floor and the splattered red walls, and the dark red spray spewing out of the shower. . . .

But as Robin dropped her eyes in horror . . . as she put her hands to her ears to shut out the sounds of Claudia's frenzied screams, she saw the girl at last . . .

Saw her small tight body huddled on the tiles in the corner . . .

Saw her hair, her face, every inch of her pale, pale skin soaked and smeared with blood.

12

"Robin! Robin, are you in there?"

Someone's calling me, but I'm dreaming—I must be dreaming—trapped in the worst nightmare I've ever had and Claudia's here with me and neither of us can get out—

"Robin!"

The voice shouted again, and it was familiar somehow. And something was pounding, loud and heavy and relentless, and as it hammered through Robin's brain, she felt herself come slowly back into focus.

"Help! Somebody help us!"

She dived under the gushing red spray and grabbed Claudia, hauling her to her feet, dragging her out of the shower.

"Oh, Claudia—oh, Claudia—you're all right —you're going to be fine!"

She was babbling and grabbing towels, wrapping Claudia up, wiping the girl's face and hair. And the whole time Claudia was like a mechanical doll, staring, just staring—

"Robin!" the voice shouted again. "I'm coming in!"

Somehow she remembered that she wasn't dressed herself, and as the door crashed open, Robin managed to grab another towel and crouch down beside Claudia on one of the benches.

"My God," Walt murmured, and he seemed strangely frozen as he stood there beside them and stared.

"The shower," Robin said. "Go look in the shower."

"Are you all right?"

"Yes, but I think Claudia might be in shock. Please hurry!"

As Robin put her arms around Claudia and slowly rocked her, she heard the water go off in the room beyond. A second later Walt reappeared and knelt down beside them, wiping his hands on his jeans and gazing anxiously into Claudia's blank face.

"Claudia," he said gently. "Everything's okay."

He raised one hand and touched her forehead. Without warning Claudia gasped and made a choking sound, and as Robin pulled back in alarm, Walt grabbed Claudia's shoulders and gave her a firm shake.

"Okay, Claudia, okay. Nothing's going to happen, you're safe."

"Blood!" she gasped, and her eyes were wild and terrified. "I told you she wanted me—I told you I'd be next—"

"It's not blood," Walt said, and as Robin stared at him, he shook his head emphatically and repeated himself. "It's not blood. Understand? Just water. Just colored water, that's all it is."

"What are you talking about?" Robin whispered.

Claudia's face was ghostly white beneath smears of red. She was shaking violently, and as Robin reached over to take her hand, she realized she was shaking just as badly herself.

"Something rigged up in the shower head." Walt's glance slid toward the other room and then back again to Robin.

"Looks like some kind of red powder or something. It's hard to tell exactly—what's left up in there is kind of syrupy now. Just turn the water on . . . instant blood. Or whatever your imagination wants to call it."

"I can't believe someone would do something like that!" Robin said furiously, close to tears.

"Believe it. Someone did."

Walt stood up and gestured toward the main door of the locker room. "Where is everyone, anyway? How come you two were here all alone?"

"We couldn't have been here alone. Miss Nelson never leaves until she's sure all the girls are gone."

"Well, I saw her in the office on my way. She looked pretty upset. Something about an emergency call, but when she got there, nobody was on the line."

Robin felt as if all her strength had drained away. She stared at Walt, and then she stared at the floor.

"Why were *you* here?" she finally asked, but before Walt could answer, another voice spoke from the hall doorway.

"I asked him to help me look for Claudia," Parker said. "I was supposed to give her a ride home, but she never showed up."

At last Claudia seemed to rouse. In slow motion she turned toward the door, and her vacant eyes came to life.

"I wasn't supposed to ride with you."

"You don't remember?" Parker looked surprised. "This morning—last thing before you left the house—you said you needed a ride home."

"I didn't." Claudia shook her head. "I never said that."

Parker shrugged. "She doesn't remember. As usual. What can I say?"

"He said he didn't know where to look for Claudia," Walt went on, talking to Robin. "I thought maybe you might know where she was. So I took a chance you hadn't left the gym yet."

"I never said that," Claudia mumbled. Her eyes moved from Parker to a wet spot on the floor. "I never did."

Parker's mouth moved in a sheepish grin. He shrugged his shoulders.

"If you don't mind," Robin said stiffly, "we'd like to get dressed."

"Don't let us stop you," Parker said amiably.

Walt flushed slightly and glanced away, as though just realizing the girls didn't have their clothes on.

"I'll see if Miss Nelson's still around," he said. "She should know what happened so someone can check it out."

"You do that," Parker said solemnly. "I'll stay right here and keep an eye on the girls. Just to make sure they're safe."

Robin's mouth opened with an angry retort, but before she could speak, Walt caught Parker neatly by the collar and spun him around, slamming the door smoothly behind them. It didn't take Robin any time to get dressed, but Claudia was a different matter. The other girl was still trembling so badly that she could hardly get into her clothes, and Robin had to help her.

"You know, don't you?" Robin said firmly as Claudia picked up her purse and started for the door. "You know that what happened in there wasn't supernatural—it didn't have anything to do with your mother?"

Claudia looked back at her with that vacuous stare.

"It was a horrible joke that someone thought would be funny. You *know* that, don't you?" Robin persisted.

"And was that someone hiding in thin air and calling for help?" Claudia asked calmly. "I know you heard it . . . you had to have heard it." She hesitated, and then she took a step toward Robin, peering earnestly into her face. "It's no use. I'm fated. Nothing you or anyone can do is going to change what's meant to be."

"Claudia . . ." Robin begged, but the other girl walked out of the room. Robin hurried to catch up, but as she neared the doorway to the gym, a dark figure suddenly stepped out to block her way.

"What you doin' in here, little girl?"

Roy Skaggs touched one hand to his forehead in a mock display of courtesy, and then he slouched over his dirty mop.

"You ain't supposed to be in here. It's the weekend. It's party time. Unless"—he grinned—"you was plannin' to have a party with me."

Robin's eyes darted frantically over his shoulder, searching the gym, looking for Walt. *Where did everyone go?*

"Did anyone else come in here a while ago?" she asked bluntly.

"Yeah. Me."

Robin ignored his sarcasm. "Just in the last half hour. Someone who might have gone into the girls' locker room? Did you hear someone talking? Or laughing?"

"Talking *and* laughing." He chuckled now. "I'm a pretty funny guy."

"Someone was calling for help," Robin said, struggling to control her temper.

"That was me calling for help." Skaggs laughed harder. "Help me clean! Help me mop!" He leaned forward with a sleazy grin, then went suddenly sober. "I don't know nothin' about laughin' and callin' for help. I just clean up the goddamn place. Clean up after stupid spoiled kids like you."

"Robin!"

To Robin's relief, she saw Claudia and Walt come up behind Skaggs. He turned slowly and fixed them with a sneer as Robin pushed past and followed them out to the parking lot.

"Talk about the lowest life form," Robin murmured, and Walt turned with a look of amusement.

"I think he was flirting with you," he deadpanned.

"Where's Parker?" Claudia glanced nervously around the lot, but Walt shook his head.

"He left. He said he felt unwanted."

"So how do we get home?" Robin said worriedly. "I'm not sure Claudia can walk."

"I picked up my car at lunch." Walt touched Robin's shoulder and steered her toward the far end of the lot. "I can drive both of you."

"To my house," Claudia said quickly. "You are coming, aren't you?" She looked pleadingly at Robin, and the other girl nodded.

"Sure I am." And then at Walt's polite look of

curiosity she added, "I have a job there after school. At Claudia's house."

"Oh," he said. "That's nice."

Robin waited for the questions, but they never came.

Claudia was silent all the way home. Robin stared out the window. She could feel Walt's eyes on her from time to time, but still he kept quiet.

"Thanks," Robin said as she and Claudia got out at the Manorwood gates. She leaned in Walt's window, her voice serious. "I really mean that."

"I know you do." The corners of Walt's mouth twitched. "But you and I still need to have a talk."

Robin nodded. She started after Claudia, hesitated, then hurried back to the car.

"Would you like to come by the house tonight? My mom goes to her exercise class about seven—I could fix hamburgers or something."

Walt stared at her.

"You like Chinese?" he said at last.

Surprised, Robin nodded.

"Then I'll bring Chinese," he said, easing the car forward. "See you at seven."

Robin caught up with Claudia, and they walked the rest of the way to the house. Just as they started in the front door, Parker's sports car squealed into the drive and he hopped out, greeting them with a wave.

"Glad to see you got home okay. I guess Walt wasn't afraid to let Claudia in his car."

Before Robin could answer, Parker stepped back, looked Claudia up and down, and gave a long low whistle.

"Wow, Claudia, you're gonna have to do something about these attacks from the netherworld."

Claudia looked as if she was going to cry. Robin glared at her tormentor.

"Stop it, Parker, that's not funny."

"It's never funny when Claudia has one of her confrontations with the dead. Is it, Claudia?" He grabbed the front door and held it open, standing back to let them pass. "Now you've even got Robin believing it. And I thought she was such a nice, sensible girl."

"Go to hell," Claudia muttered.

Parker fell back dramatically and put his hand to his heart.

"I'm doomed!" he wailed. "The curse is upon me!"

Robin couldn't stand it anymore. Furiously she whirled on him, her face inches from his own.

"Haven't you ever been scared?" she lashed out. "Haven't you ever been so terrified that you couldn't get through a day without expecting something horrible to happen?"

His grin faded. He looked her levelly in the eye.

"Yes. Living with Claudia is scary. Living with her mother was terrifying."

"I hate you—" Claudia's voice broke, and she ran into the house, leaving Parker gazing after her.

"You really are unbelievable," Robin threw at him, then went inside, slamming the door in his face.

She hadn't gotten very far when something grabbed her from behind and spun her around. Before she could even scream, Parker dragged her through the nearest doorway, tossed her onto a couch, and stood over her, hands clenched at his sides.

Robin was so shocked all she could do was stare.

She watched as he strode to a chair, dragged it across the floor until it was directly opposite her, and then sat down, looking her coldly in the eye.

"Now," he said calmly. She had never heard his voice so low and dangerous. "I think you need to be enlightened a little about our special and wonderful family."

"I don't want to know about your family. I don't want to know about your personal life—"

"Oh, I think you do. As a matter of fact, I think you *should*—because maybe then you'll understand a little more clearly why things are the way they are."

"I don't want to hear this." Robin put her hands over her ears, but Parker forced them back down.

"Claudia's mother was a witch—did you know that?"

Robin drew herself up stiffly. "A medium and a witch are hardly the same thing—"

"I'm not talking about the kind that rides a broom. She was evil, Robin. She was selfish and self-centered and only out for herself. She was a fraud. She preyed on the grief of innocent people and took their money and lied to them!"

"How do you know that?"

"Because I watched her work. Long before she ever married my father. She had a business not far from where we lived—a tourist trap. She had regular customers and held séances for them so they could contact their dear departed loved ones. But she just made things up! None of the stuff she ever told them was true."

"Then if it wasn't true, why did people keep coming back to her?"

"People need to believe things when they're grieving so badly. Just like my father. He was so lost after my mother died, he believed everything Lillith told him. And then she told him he'd never have to be lonely again—that someone special and beautiful was coming into his life. And then he married *her.*"

Robin looked away, her face stony.

"Look, Parker, I believe there's an afterlife and that some people have the gift to reach into it. I don't believe every spiritualist is a fake and just out to take advantage of people."

"But you didn't know Lillith."

"And did you? Really?"

"Robin, she worked for us, right there in our house, before my mother ever died. She had lots of time to study my father, to know what he liked and didn't, to learn just how to manipulate him. I had a lot of time to see how Lillith operated."

"What do you mean, she worked in your house?"

Parker sat back and ran one hand impatiently through his hair.

"She didn't make enough money with that phony business of hers, so she did other jobs on the side. She used to clean our house. In fact, she used to bring Claudia to help her. Lillith got to be very good friends with my family . . . except for Grandfather. Lillith knew how much my mother liked flowers, so she started bringing seeds and cuttings for the garden. Lillith knew how much my father admired art, so she began doing paintings for him."

Parker glanced at the macabre portrait by the door.

"After my mother died, Lillith held séances for my father. To help him make contact with my mother." His face went grim. "He was so lost without her, he believed everything Lillith told him."

Robin watched the anger in Parker's eyes. She wanted to look away, but she couldn't.

"How . . . how *did* your mother die?" she asked gently.

"We lived out on the ocean, but she drove into the village every Thursday to shop. It was a dangerous road—narrow with lots of steep curves—but she liked to go alone. She always said it was her thinking time." Parker faltered for a moment. He dropped his gaze, and his voice went quiet. "No one was with her when it happened—so no one will ever really know, I suppose. She must have lost control of the car somehow. She went off the road and down an incline."

His eyes lifted. He looked at Robin, and his voice shook ever so slightly.

"The car landed . . . very far down. And burned."

Parker stood up. He walked slowly to the mantel, and he stared into the fireplace.

"They said she was killed instantly but . . ."

He stopped.

He cleared his throat, and he kept his back to Robin.

"But she must have known," he whispered. "She must have known what was happening all the way down. . . ."

Robin covered her face with her hands. She tasted tears, but as Parker turned and started back toward her, she wiped them quickly away.

"Lillith was never like her," Parker said, his voice growing hard. "Never good or kind. Lillith *used* my father, Robin. She only wanted his money. I know she didn't love him. I know she never did."

Robin said nothing. She watched a range of emotions struggle over Parker's face, and after a while she leaned toward him.

"Parker, you and I are really talking about the same thing, aren't we? We're both saying that

Claudia's mother is dangerous and that she has powers—"

"She doesn't have any powers," Parker interrupted. "The only powers she has are in Claudia's mind."

"Claudia is *terrified!*" Robin insisted. "Nobody could be that terrified and be making it up!"

"Claudia," Parker said slowly, "is crazy. Pure and simple. Don't believe her, Robin. Don't trust her."

"Parker, I was there. I've *been* there—with her—more than once! I know what happened."

His eyes narrowed. "The storage room, you mean? Last night? Embarrassing yourself over some stupid curtains soaking in a bathtub—"

"But what about today in the showers? I heard someone, too—I thought it was blood, too—"

"Oh, come on, Robin, how often do you think kids rig up jokes in locker rooms!"

"But there've been other things—"

"What other things? I want you to tell me each and every thing that's happened to Claudia, and I bet I can explain each and every one of them away!"

Robin glared at him, too upset to argue anymore.

"I have to go," she said abruptly. She stood up and took a deep breath. "I have a lot of work to do."

"Suit yourself." Parker watched her a moment, then took her place on the couch. He leaned back slowly and crossed his long legs out in front of him. "But don't say I didn't warn you." He smiled.

"I don't like threats," Robin said.

"No? Then you'd better be careful. Before you know it, Lillith will be coming for you, too."

He started laughing.

He laughed and laughed, and as Robin stormed out into the hallway, the sound of Parker's voice echoed over and over again in her ears.

He could hardly keep her mind on

13

She could hardly keep her mind on her work.

Alone in the study, Robin kept drifting off, catching herself gazing into the fire, only to realize that lapses of time had passed and that she'd been sitting there holding her pencil uselessly in her hand.

She managed to get through only one more carton of books when old Mr. Swanson came shuffling in, carrying a tea tray.

"Ah, there you are!" he exclaimed, wagging his bushy head. "The girl of my dreams!"

It was even an effort for Robin to smile. Herk set the tray down on the desk and poured from a chipped china pot.

"Mint tea," he announced, handing her a cup and saucer. "Good for what ails you. Which, by the look of you this afternoon, seems to be considerable."

Robin looked guilty. "I didn't think it showed."

"Maybe not to most people. But yes, to me, yes." He eased himself into a chair and frowned at her. "I believe our boy is smitten with you."

Unconsciously Robin stiffened. "Hmph."

"No? Disagree? Or just not reciprocated?"

Robin shook her head, but before she could speak, Herk went on.

"He's brilliant. I've said it before and I'll keep saying it to anyone who'll listen! He's handsome and he's sharp. Not like that limp little Claudia. Know what she reminds me of? Spaghetti. A piece of spaghetti all boiled away. Limp and white and boring."

Robin stared at the floor. A picture flashed through her mind—Claudia huddled in the shower, covered in red.

"She's terrified, Mr. Swanson," Robin said.

"Herk!" he barked at her.

"Herk. Claudia is terrified. Of something. Of her mother. Of her mother coming back or—"

"What in blazes are you talking about? That girl always has some paranoia or another. Why, back in our old place she was taking a tray full of medicine every single day. A walking pharmacy, that girl. Stuff to sleep, stuff to wake up, stuff for bad dreams, stuff for anemia, stuff for—ah, well"—he made an impatient gesture in the air—"what does it matter? Puny stock, that's what I say. Why in God's name my stupid son ever married her disgusting mother is beyond me!"

"Why do you say that?" Robin asked seriously.

"Say what?"

"Why do you hate Lillith so much?"

"She bewitched him!" Herk's face screwed up, and he fairly spat out the words. "Bewitched him, pure and simple! Now, Parker's mother—there was a beauty if ever I saw one—sweet and simple and loving. Not a sorceress like that Lillith. And Lillith was a common person, to boot. Should never have been involved with our family at all."

"But . . . your son must have loved her."

"He *thought* he loved her, but Gardner's never been known for his great perceptions! That wasn't love, what he felt for Lillith—that was desperation! Thank God I still hold the purse strings in this family—no telling what idiotic thing my stupid son might pull next! After he made the decision to marry Lillith, how could I ever trust him with the family fortune? No, they're all lucky I'm still around to keep this crazy family on its feet."

Robin took a sip of tea and leaned back in her chair.

"You really love Parker, don't you?" she asked softly and noticed how the old man's eyes took on a tender sort of shine at the mention of his grandson's name.

"Oh, I know he's brash—rude sometimes—

but so was I when I was young and handsome."
Herk leaned forward, a conspiratorial twinkle in
his eye. "I turned heads and broke hearts!"

Robin had to smile. "I don't doubt that for a
minute."

"Well, *don't* doubt it, 'cause I *did!* Parker has
the brains—he just doesn't know how to use
them all yet. He's going to *be* someone. He's
going to keep this family name going. He knows
how to *work* people—*charm* people—he can be
a *very* persuasive young man. Yes, I know you can
call it insincerity if you want to, but I don't call it
that at all! I call it *smart!* In this day and age it's
important to get people on your side. That's how
you *build.* That's how you *survive.*"

"He doesn't like Claudia very much, does he?"

"Claudia? Hates her! Despises her! Well, can't
blame him, can I? My stupid son wants to split
up Parker's inheritance and give the girl half—
what in blazes is Gardner thinking! I'll tell you
what he's thinking—*nothing!* He never thinks at
all! That was *Lillith's* idea—the witch! *She* put
that stupid idea in my stupid son's head! Well, I
forbid it! Claudia already gets Lillith's share, and
that's *all* the Swanson money she's ever going to
get! Gardner wants to put her in the will—well,
okay! But we'll *all* have to die first before Claudia
gets *one—more—penny!* Parker will do great
things with that money. Run the family business.
Carry on the family name. Improve what I
started all those years ago. Not like that wimpy
son of mine who can't do anything right."

Herk leaned back, a dreamy look on his face.

"Parker. He's my hope. My future. He *deserves* the inheritance he'll come into—not like Claudia. She didn't have to do *anything* to deserve her money. Just be here. Just have a witch for a mother. So if Parker hates her, I say fine! All she does is run around and upset everybody with that wild imagination of hers. Should have been a writer or something. Then someone else could pay her for making things up."

"So you believe Parker really hates Claudia because of the money?" Robin asked seriously.

Herk scowled. "Not just the money. Everything. The money's just part of it. Mostly he just hates her 'cause she's Claudia. What better reason?"

Robin set her saucer down. "And you think . . . you think it really *is* just her imagination?"

"Listen to me." Herk stood up and began pacing, his hands folded behind his stooped back. "Ever since Lillith died, Claudia's believed her mother's coming back for her. It's guilt, I tell you, nothing but guilt. Want to know what I think?"

Robin knew he would tell her regardless, so she nodded.

"I think Claudia was *glad* when her mother disappeared! Why, I think Claudia was so downright overjoyed that she stood right there on that beach and prayed to all the gods of the sea that Lillith would be washed clean out to kingdom come! But then"—Herk's voice lowered to a stage whisper, and he leaned in close to Robin's chair—"then when she actually *saw* Lillith—laid out all white and drowned and dead on those rocks—she was so horrified at her own feelings, she went straight out of her mind!"

Herk rocked back on his heels, looking immensely pleased with himself.

"The night after Lillith killed herself, Claudia woke us all up screaming. Said Lillith was standing down there on the beach calling for help, with shells and seaweed in her hair, waving her arms all around, telling Claudia to follow her! Does that sound like a sane person to you?" He snorted and jabbed a finger in the air for emphasis. "That girl is crazy as a bedbug."

The clock on the desk chimed softly, and Robin jumped.

"I should get home," she said. "Do you want me to come tomorrow?"

"You mean you don't have a hot date this weekend?" Herk teased. "You mean you'd rather be with me?"

"You're the best hot date I could think of." Robin grinned, and he hugged her and walked her to the door.

"It's dark," he said, scowling out at the chilly night. "I'll get Parker to take you—"

"No," Robin said quickly. "Please don't bother. It's not far."

"But—"

"Really. It'll only take me a few minutes to get home from here."

She gathered her things together before he could protest, and then she hurried down the drive toward the gate. It felt as if a storm was brewing. A restless wind lashed the bare trees, and what few leaves remained on their branches now swirled wildly in the air. Robin brushed her hair back from her face and stopped suddenly, her heart in her throat.

A noise? Or just the wind?

A footstep?

Quit being so jumpy—it's just been a strange day—too many questions—too many suspicions . . .

She forced herself to think about home and Walt coming over. She forced herself to think about that funny way he had of smiling and how he already seemed to know what she was going to tell him tonight—

There it is again.

Robin froze, her hands clenched in her pockets.

Between the moaning of the wind and the flailing of the trees, it was impossible to hear anything clearly. She shielded her eyes and looked up into the sky. A glob of yellow moon showed ghostly behind torn ribbons of black clouds. Strange shadows leapt around her like dark spirits in torment.

Come on, Robin, quit scaring yourself.

She began to walk faster. Her sneakers thudded softly on the driveway, crackling leaves underfoot, snapping twigs. The wind wasn't

moaning anymore, but sighing—a haunting
sound . . . a sad sound—

"Robin," it sighed . . . *"help me . . ."*

Robin broke into a run. Her breath was ragged
in her throat, and her heart felt as if it was going
to explode. The driveway seemed to have ac-
quired a whole new series of twists and turns
through the trees, seemed to have become an
impossible maze that led nowhere. Dangerous
shadows lurked around her—invisible watchers
waited for her to fall. Limbs reached down and
snatched at her, and she screamed as one caught
her by the hair.

Robin couldn't move.

In her terror the more she tried to free herself,
the more her hair tangled in the tree branch.
Jerking and pulling, she only succeeded in trap-
ping herself more. At last she managed to tilt her
head back and grab for the limb.

But it wasn't the limb she felt beneath her
fingertips.

It was a badly scarred face.

"Well, looka here," a voice hissed, and as
Robin screamed, she felt slow, sour breath sweep
over her.

"Yessiree, just look here what we have."

Eyes wide, Robin saw Skaggs's face only inches
from her own, a sleazy grin spreading over his
lips. She gave one hard tug and heard him laugh.

"You're just makin' it worse, strugglin' like
that," Skaggs scolded gently. "You're just gettin'
yourself in a hell of a mess."

From Robin's twisted angle she saw his arm move out from his side, saw him lean a shovel up against a tree.

"Hear that wind?" he murmured. "It's so loud, you could scream and scream and probably nobody would hear."

To Robin's horror she felt his hand on her hair . . . on her cheek . . . sliding down the side of her neck . . .

"Stop it!" she cried. "Let me go!"

"Why should I?" he whispered, his lips against her ear. "When you're so nice and helpless this way?"

"No—"

"You should be nicer to me, little girl. You and I could make some kind of a . . . partnership, hmmm?"

"Get away from her, Skaggs."

Robin screamed again as a tall shadow disentangled itself from the trees. She felt Skaggs go rigid, and in the next second he shoved her away.

"I didn't mean nothin'," he was practically whining now, fumbling with her hair, trying to pull it from the branch while she struggled to get away. "I didn't mean nothin' . . . I was only tryin' to help—"

"Don't ever touch her," the voice said again.

It was a cold voice . . . a frightening voice.

With one final jerk Robin felt her hair come free.

She looked up into Parker's angry stare, and then she turned and ran.

14

Afterward Robin didn't remember getting home.

One minute she was caught in Parker's merciless gaze, and the next she was inside her front door, leaning against it, gasping for breath. She didn't know how long she stood there, shaking, trying to clear her mind, trying to collect herself, trying to make sense of what had happened. . . .

She could still hear Skaggs's oily voice, smell the liquor on his breath, feel the sleazy touch of his hand—and when she closed her eyes and tried to force the images away, she could still see the shovel leaning up against the tree, and Parker materializing out of the shadows. . . .

What were they doing out there?

And if Parker hadn't shown up . . . what—

Something thudded beside her head, and Robin jumped back into the hallway with a scream.

For a moment she'd forgotten she was leaning against the front door. She hadn't expected someone to knock on the other side.

Walt . . .

"Who is it?" Her voice was shaking so badly she could hardly speak.

For a moment no one answered.

And then, hesitantly, "Robin? It's me. Walt."

She flung the door wide and stood there staring at him. And the next thing she knew, he was in the hall and his arms were around her, and he was searching her face with an anxious frown.

"What's wrong? What's happened?"

"A lot. I don't know." She was shaking her head and had a hold of his arms, leading him back into the kitchen. She saw him nod and shrug out of his jacket, and then they were standing beneath the bright lights, and things were beginning to come back into normal focus once more.

"A lot," Robin said again. "I don't even know where to start."

Walt slipped his jacket over the back of a chair.

"How about with egg rolls?"

Robin looked blank. "What?"

"I've always found," he went on calmly, producing a sack that Robin hadn't even noticed, "that it's best to start with egg rolls. And then get on to the really important stuff. Like the chow mein."

She watched as he put the sack on the counter and began pulling out little white containers.

"Sit down," he said quietly. "Before you fall down."

Robin sat. She sat and she stared while Walt arranged all the cartons on the table and folded paper towels into napkins and pulled cans of soda from the refrigerator.

"Pepsi okay?"

Robin nodded.

She watched as he sat down across from her. He rested his arms calmly on the tabletop and leaned slightly forward and brushed his long hair back from his forehead.

"Okay," he said. "You'd better tell me."

"You'll think I'm crazy," Robin replied. "And actually . . . *I* think I might be crazy."

"Well"—he sighed—"better to find out now before this goes any deeper."

"What?"

"Never mind. Just tell me."

She did. She started with the ad on the bulletin board and didn't stop until her latest encounter with Skaggs and Parker. The whole time she talked, Walt sat there with his unshakable stare, only moving one time to take a sip of his Pepsi. When Robin finished, she sank back in her chair, let out a sigh, and waited for him to say something insightful.

"I think you should eat something," was what he came up with. "It'll help calm you down."

"I was expecting some words of wisdom," Robin said, sounding disappointed.

"Wisdom. Well." Walt also leaned back in his

chair. He put one hand to his chin and thought a moment. "It's not good to rush into wisdom. I have to think about it first."

"I'm scared," Robin said.

"For who?"

"Claudia mostly. I think someone's after her."

"But someone definitely alive, I'd guess."

"Then you don't believe in powers beyond the grave?"

"Sure I believe. But I'm not so certain it's just power driving that black car and turning off lights in houses and playing parlor tricks."

Robin nodded. "All I know is that Claudia's in danger. She thinks she's doomed to follow the fate of her mother, and from what I've seen lately, she might be right. The rest of the family hated Lillith—and they seem to hate Claudia, too."

"And say she's crazy."

"Yes." Robin nodded sadly.

"And what do you say?"

"The poor thing is terrified. I would be, too." Robin leaned forward and looked at him pleadingly. "Can't we tell the police?"

"Oh, so we're back to this again. And I still say, tell them what?"

Robin frowned and settled back again. "Our . . . thoughts."

"Hmmm . . . I'm not sure they'd consider that hard, fast evidence."

Robin frowned. "I just wonder what Skaggs is doing around there anyway."

"Besides being a pervert?"

"You're right. It is his greatest talent."

"Well, the family's new—what do you expect?" Walt shrugged. "Skaggs came cheap, and they haven't quite discovered his impeccable character yet." He held up an egg roll and studied it closely as Robin thought out loud.

"I can't imagine why Parker would be out there with Skaggs."

"Are you sure Parker *was* with Skaggs?" he asked. "Or did he just happen to show up about that time?"

"Like the way he just *happened* to show up the day Claudia fell down the stairs? And the way he just *happened* to be looking for Claudia today?"

"He could be telling the truth. Then won't you feel heartless?" Walt scolded.

Robin considered this a moment. "He did seem pretty upset tonight. About Skaggs touching me, I mean."

"I bet," Walt said easily. "He thinks you're pretty hot."

Robin looked startled, her cheeks going bright pink. Walt reached casually for the soy sauce.

"What did you say?" Robin demanded.

"You heard me," Walt said. "It's not hard to figure out."

"How can you say such a thing?" Robin sputtered. "With his arrogance and his—his—"

"All right, you don't have to convince *me* how you feel about him." The corners of Walt's mouth twitched. "I'm just telling you what—as a *guy*—I know. And I *know* Parker Swanson would like to be . . . *involved* with you."

"This is so silly." Robin crossed her arms over her chest. "I don't want to talk about this anymore."

"We don't have to. What would you like to talk about?"

"You can be so frustrating!"

"Um-hmm. It's one of my strong points." Walt broke open a fortune cookie. "This is yours. I'll read it to you."

"I don't want to hear it," Robin said, sulking. "Not if it's anything like the rest of my life these days."

"You're going to be very rich and marry an old man named Herk," Walt recited solemnly.

Robin tried to glare at him but failed miserably.

She groaned. "I don't want to laugh. I'm not in the mood. You're not taking any of this seriously."

"On the contrary, I'm taking this *very* seriously. I think someone could be in danger here, but I'm not sure it's Claudia."

Surprised, Robin looked up.

"No? Then who?"

For a long moment Walt gazed at her.

Robin watched him reach slowly into his shirt pocket and pull out a piece of paper. He leaned across the table and held it out to her, but she only stared.

"What's that?" she whispered.

"It was on your front door when I got here tonight," he said. "Didn't you see it?"

Robin couldn't speak. She could only shake her head.

"Which means either you were so upset that you just didn't notice . . ." He paused and took a deep breath. "Or that someone—whoever it was—put it there *after* you came inside."

Robin felt her skin go cold.

"I . . . I can't read it," she said.

"You don't have to. I already did."

Walt crumpled the paper in his fist and laid it on the table between them.

"It says . . . 'Stay away from Claudia or you'll be next.'"

15

The room seemed to recede around her.

Robin gripped the edge of the table until Walt's face came slowly back into focus.

"We have to go to the police" was all she could think of to say.

"We can't go to the police," Walt said again, just as patiently. "They'll say it's just kids playing jokes on each other. Which it might be. Except it's not funny."

"So . . . so does this mean"—Robin swallowed hard—"that someone might try to . . . kill me or something?"

"I think someone is trying to *scare* you. Just like they're trying to scare Claudia."

"Well, they're doing a good job. I'm scared."

"You don't have to be scared. Nothing's going to happen to you."

Robin stared at him. "How can you be so sure?"

"Because I won't let it," Walt said simply. "Now." He lifted his eyes to the ceiling, deep in thought for a long moment. "Why would someone want Claudia to think her mother's after her?"

"To . . ." Robin shrugged. "I don't know. To make her scared, like you said. To make her feel . . . stalked. Terrorized."

"Try insane."

"What?"

"To make Claudia think she's losing her mind. Just like her mother supposedly did."

"You said 'supposedly.' You think maybe Lillith wasn't crazy?"

"Is Claudia? We don't *know* what happened when Lillith was alive, but if someone keeps trying to brainwash Claudia into thinking her dead mother's after her, why *shouldn't* Claudia think she's insane? Or more important"—Walt frowned—"why shouldn't everyone *else* think Claudia's insane?"

"You mean . . ." Robin's mind was stumbling, trying to keep up. "You mean if people think Claudia is insane—"

"They'd have to *prove* it first. But say they did. If she's declared incompetent, what could happen?"

"They could lock her up? They could put her somewhere? An institution?"

"And what would she stand to lose?"

Robin looked baffled. "You've lost *me.*"

"Family support? Approval? Dowry? Inheritance? Allowance? Any of those ring a bell?"

Robin sat up straighter. "There is some kind of an inheritance—something split between her and Parker, that they're supposed to get when they turn eighteen."

The grave implication hung in the air between them. Robin rubbed a chill slowly from her arms.

"Parker?" she said slowly. "Then you think . . . *Parker* is trying to make Claudia look insane so she doesn't get to inherit her part of the family fortune?"

Walt shook his head. "I don't know. I'm just speculating. We can only work with the pieces of the puzzle we have. There may be hundreds more pieces we don't even know about yet."

"Well, I don't like being one of those pieces," Robin shuddered. "Just because I happened to answer an ad on the bulletin board. In fact, I think I'll go over to Manorwood first thing in the morning and quit."

Walt nodded. "That seems the sensible thing to do."

Robin nodded in unison, then stopped and sagged in her chair.

"I can't quit."

"Why not?"

"And just leave Claudia there with that . . . that vulture Parker?"

"We don't know if Parker has anything to do with this or not. Remember? We're just tossing out theories here."

"Stop being so fair," Robin grumbled. "And so nice."

"I'm just trying to consider all the angles."

"Walt, she doesn't have anybody! I'm the only one right now who knows something's going on—the only one who *believes* her! I mean, I've been right there with her, and I've seen things happen! I can't just go off and abandon her!" Robin crossed her arms on the tabletop and buried her face against them. "Don't you have any other theories you'd like to toss out?"

"Only one," Walt said.

"And what's that?"

"I strongly suspect Claudia's not the only reason you're keeping that job."

Robin looked startled. "What are you talking about?"

Walt smiled. "Vultures."

Saturday dawned dismal and rainy, with stormclouds boiling in a pewter-gray sky. Robin stood at the window a long time and stared out at the steady drizzle. She hadn't been able to get Walt's remarks out of her mind, and she'd gone over them relentlessly all night long. It infuriated her, his insinuation that she might have any sort of positive feelings for Parker. *Imagine—Parker Swanson!* After all his blatant arrogance and conceit—after all the things he'd obviously done to Claudia to keep her vulnerable and upset! Robin fumed just thinking about it. So what if Walt thought Parker cared about her—so what if Claudia said Parker talked about her! *I don't care—he doesn't mean a thing to me!*

In desperation she picked up the phone and dialed Faye. She'd waited too long to share all this with her friend—she needed to hear Faye's jokes, needed to hear Faye tell her that she was being silly, that she was blowing everything way out of proportion as usual.

"Sorry, hon, but Zak picked her up early this morning," Faye's mother apologized. "Can I give her a message?"

Robin's heart sank. "Just . . . no. No message."

She felt alone and depressed. For the hundredth time she wished she'd never heard of Manorwood. For the hundredth time she made up her mind to march over there and quit her job.

But then the image of Claudia's face came into her mind.

She saw Claudia's face and she heard Claudia's voice, Claudia's terror, Claudia's confusion, and Robin felt racked with guilt.

So she was surprised as she stood there at the window and heard the doorbell ring. It was only eight o'clock, and she wasn't expecting anyone. And certainly not Claudia, whom she found standing on her porch when she opened the door.

"You're soaking wet!" Robin exclaimed, dragging the girl inside. "Come have some coffee."

"Are you alone?" Claudia asked nervously.

"Alone? Well, Mom drove up for some parent's thing at my brother's college, but—"

"I mean, is Parker here?" Claudia glanced around the entryway as though she expected her brother to pop out from the wall and terrify her.

"No, why would Parker be here?"

"I thought I heard him last night," Claudia looked a little sheepish. "I thought I heard him tell Grandfather that he was going to come and see you this morning. I don't want to be here if *he's* going to be here."

Robin felt a tingle of apprehension but kept her voice calm. "No, he's not here. Why? What's wrong?"

"I found something this morning," Claudia whispered. "Something . . . horrible."

Robin stared at the pitiful little figure dripping all over the hall rug. Claudia's face was gaunt and haggard, and she looked as if she might collapse at any moment.

"What was it?" Robin asked gently.

"A . . . a hand."

Robin stared at her.

"A hand," Claudia said again. "On my pillow."

"You . . . found . . ."

"You act like you don't believe me!" Claudia cried. "You act like you don't believe me, but it's true! I woke up and it was there on my pillow—

right beside my head! And all this blood—my mother's blood, I tell you—my mother's hand!"

"Oh, Claudia—"

"You sound just like them! Humoring me! And all the time you don't really believe I saw what I saw!" Claudia's voice broke, and she swayed dangerously. Robin reached out and caught her and ushered her into the kitchen. She sat Claudia down in a chair and poured her a strong cup of coffee.

"Drink this," Robin ordered. "It'll make you feel better." *A hand . . . a hand. Some kind of rubber contraption—some Halloween prop— Parker must have put it there while she was asleep—*

"I screamed," Claudia said in a weary monotone. "I screamed and I screamed. I ran out to the hall, but I couldn't find anybody. I ran downstairs and finally found Winifred, and I brought her back to my room. . . ." She lowered her eyes, blinking back tears. "But it wasn't there anymore. The hand. It just . . ." her voice faded, "wasn't there."

Of course it wasn't, Robin thought bitterly, *Parker hid it somewhere,* but aloud she said, "Claudia, are you sure it wasn't—you know— part of a costume or something—"

"It was *real!*" Claudia clenched her teeth, and her chin lifted defiantly. "I think I can tell a real hand from a fake hand, Robin. I'm not that crazy yet!"

"No, Claudia, that's not what I meant at all—"

"It'll be soon, though," Claudia murmured, and Robin had to lean forward to hear her.

"Soon?"

"Yes." The girl nodded mechanically. "I can feel it. She'll come for me soon. She'll come for me, and this time when it happens, I won't be able to escape like I have all those other times. This time"—her voice trembled—"she'll have me at last."

Robin sat down on the other side of the table. Her knees felt suddenly shaky, and her cup trembled in her hand.

"I know how it'll happen," Claudia whispered.

"Stop talking like that," Robin said, but Claudia didn't seem to hear.

"Because . . . sometimes I dream about it." Claudia's lips barely moved. "I'm standing on a high, high cliff. And *she's* there—down at the bottom—holding out her arms to me. 'Jump, Claudia,' she says, 'jump and I'll catch you.'"

Robin reached for the girl's hand. It was ice cold.

"I've told my dream to Parker," Claudia's brow furrowed slightly. "And to Winifred and Grandfather. But they always tell me it's just a nightmare." She smiled softly. "I know better."

"Come on, Claudia, don't do this—"

"And you know . . ." Claudia murmured, "I don't think I'll really mind. It'll be . . . a relief." Her eyes lifted slowly, and their chilling resignation sliced straight into Robin's heart. "A relief," Claudia whispered. "No more running . . . ever again."

"I'm going to call your grandfather," Robin said. She started to get up, but Claudia's hand clamped down on her like a claw.

"Don't . . . please. You know what he'll do. He'll say you're on his side, and he'll be glad. And then he'll put me somewhere, and I couldn't bear that. Please, Robin. Please. I'd *rather* die. Really. I'd rather be with . . . with *her* . . . than locked up somewhere with strangers."

Robin gazed into Claudia's eyes. She saw their pain, their immeasurable sadness, and suddenly she felt something boil up inside her— something hot and mean and angry. *"Crazy old Claudia,"* Parker had said. *"Crazy old Claudia—"*

Biting her lip, Robin stood up and gave Claudia's hand a firm squeeze.

"You won't have to go anywhere, Claudia," she said. "I promise."

Claudia looked confused, but Robin only smiled at her.

"I have work to do," Robin said.

"You mean . . . at the house?"

"Yes, but there's something else I have to do first. Will you be all right at home for a while? Can you wait for me there?"

Claudia nodded, an obedient child. "If you want me to."

"Good. I'll come as soon as I can."

Robin watched Claudia go off down the sidewalk. She went upstairs and got dressed, and then she left the house.

But this time she didn't go straight to Manorwood.

This time she walked all the way into town and went determinedly into the police station.

16

Robin had never felt so humiliated.

As she walked slowly out of the building, she stood a moment blinking back tears, wishing she could just disappear into the cracks of the sidewalk.

Why didn't I stop to think about what I was doing? Why didn't I at least wait and talk to Faye about it first?

Because I couldn't wait for Faye to get home. And because Faye doesn't even know what's going on. And where would I even start trying to explain it all to her now?

Of course the police hadn't believed her.

Of course they'd thought she was just a stupid teenager trying to make up some crazy story, caught up in someone's idea of a joke, a victim of her own overactive imagination.

I should have listened to Walt.

She could still see the face of the policeman she'd talked to. How he'd sat there with that polite, professional smile, trying so hard to hide his amusement, leaning back in his chair, making doodles with a pencil on his tablet. She'd told him everything—just like she'd told Walt— about the accidents and all the weird things that had happened, and how she thought Parker was trying to set Claudia up to cut her out of her inheritance. Even now she couldn't believe she'd done it, couldn't believe she'd been so idiotic. She wished she could take back every single word she'd said. She wished . . .

Why didn't I listen to Walt? What have I done?

She'd heard them laughing as she'd left the station. Softly, so she wouldn't know they were making fun of her. Imagine, they were probably saying, even now—coming in with an insane story like that, and even using the Swanson name.

But you haven't been with Claudia like I have . . . you haven't seen her fear, her terror . . . you didn't listen to her this morning, all ready to die and be with her mother—

There was no way around it now—if she was going to help Claudia, she was totally on her own.

She looked up into the churning clouds and wiped rain from her cheeks. The sky was a quilted mass of black now, threaded through with jagged spurts of lightning. Robin ducked her head again as a rumble of thunder shook the air around her, and she took off down the street. The storm broke full force as she neared the gates of Manorwood. She quickened her steps, but then froze when the gates suddenly swung open and Parker's sports car sped out of the driveway. Some instinct made Robin jump back and flatten herself into the shrubbery. She was fairly certain she hadn't been noticed, but from her hiding place, she'd been able to get a good look at Parker's face.

His mouth was set in a hard line, and he was hunched down over the wheel, gripping it with both hands. His hair and his clothes looked drenched, and there was mud on his cheeks and what she could see of his jacket.

Robin stayed where she was for a long time, hardly even aware that she was soaked through to her skin. The wind was cold, but not nearly as cold as the shiver that crept through her veins and curled slowly around her heart. With an effort she forced herself on to the gates and up the drive to the house, and was just in time to meet Winifred coming out the front door.

"Oh, Miss Robin," Winifred greeted her primly, struggling to open her umbrella. "You've gotten caught in the storm!"

"It's nothing. I can dry off by the fire."

"Are you sure?" the maid fretted. "This is my day off, you know, so if you need anything, please just help yourself."

"Thanks," Robin gave a quick smile. "Is Claudia home?"

"Yes, but not feeling very well, poor little

thing." Winifred rolled her eyes and lowered her voice as she leaned toward Robin. "She's such a frail little mouse. Sometimes I—"

She broke off suddenly and straightened, as though realizing she might have confided too much.

Robin tried her best to sound casual.

"What is it, Winifred? Sometimes I worry about Claudia, too."

"Well . . ." Again the maid rolled her eyes, as if to reassure herself they weren't being spied upon. "She says she hears things—hears her mother, she says—coming for her—calling for help."

Robin nodded slowly.

"The men, oh, they never believe her," Winifred scoffed. "But *I* do! I hear Miss Lillith, just as plain as day! Miss Lillith—calling for help! Sometimes even when I'm there, right there in the room with Claudia!"

Again Robin suppressed a shiver.

"Were they close, Claudia and her mother?" she asked.

"Not hardly, no." Winifred clutched her handbag and pressed her lips tightly together. "Didn't get along at all, always *at* each other. And them looking so much alike, as you can see!" She shook her head disapprovingly. "Miss Lillith, she was always trying to get Claudia to be like her—do the things she did! She could talk to the dead, you know. She tried to teach Claudia, too, but the poor thing was always too afraid!"

"Teach her?" Robin echoed. "What do you mean?"

"You know! How to have the gift! How to contact that other world where the spirits live! But she's too timid, Miss Claudia is—she'd get scared and cry about it—so finally Miss Lillith stopped trying to force her."

Robin shook her head sadly. Was there ever anyone in Claudia's life who had really accepted her for who she was?

"She's a sweet little thing," Winifred added, seeming to pick up on Robin's thoughts. "But . . . you know . . . strange. If her mother *did* come for her, I wouldn't be a bit surprised. Do you know what I mean? I think Miss Claudia *expects* it! I think she's *ready!* Just waiting for Miss Lillith to come and take her away from this place!"

There was a creak behind them, and Winifred whirled with a gasp. The hallway was empty. Overhead the lights flickered as thunder shook the walls.

"I'd better be off if I'm going to catch that matinee!" Winifred said, and then she held out her hand to Robin. "Thank you for being a friend to Miss Claudia. She could use one, and that's no lie."

Robin watched Winifred start down the drive. As soon as the woman had vanished through the wet trees, Robin sighed and closed the door behind her.

"Claudia!" she called. "Are you here?"

Her voice echoed back gloomily, and she slipped out of her jacket.

"Claudia?"

There was no answer.

She must be resting. I'll leave her alone and get right to work.

The fire had been lit in the study, and the room was a welcome relief from the murky day outside. Robin pulled several cartons of books up to the desk and got busy.

As it had before, the room lulled her into a doze. With the fire crackling softly and the popping of the logs, with the burnished glow of the lamps and the gathering clouds beyond the window, Robin felt enclosed in a warm cocoon. Several times she nodded off and caught herself when her pen dropped from her hand. She fought to keep her eyes open, but the coziness was impossible to resist after such a restless night. At last she gave in to the temptation, cradling her head upon the desk, and she slept.

She wasn't sure what woke her.

Her eyes flew open, and as she caught a glimpse of the clock, she saw she'd been out for several hours. Her neck and back felt stiff. She groaned softly and turned her face to the other side.

She saw the odd-shaped thing as she lifted her head, but she didn't know what it was.

She saw it lying there, only inches from her cheek, and as she smelled the overpowering stench, she thought she knew now what had woken her. . . .

The hand was already in the stages of decay.

It lay there, fingers splayed out like a twisted claw, with a paintbrush wedged between them.

Dark spots had already crept over the torn flesh. . . .

Something was oozing slowly where its thumb should have been.

As Robin bolted upright and gagged, she saw Claudia suddenly appear in the doorway, rubbing sleep from her eyes, her lips forming a sad, welcoming sort of smile.

"Claudia . . ." Robin began.

Claudia's eyes jerked wide—her hands flew to her mouth and her shoulders convulsed like a macabre marionette.

And as both girls stared in horror at the thing on the desk, something whispered, something laughed a horrible laugh out of the empty shadows of the room. . . .

"No one can help you now. . . ."

17

It's a trick, Claudia, it's a trick!" Robin screamed, even though she knew the thing lying there on the desk was all too grisly, all too real—

"Oh, God, Claudia—"

She saw the girl take a step back, saw her hand grope blindly through the air as if seeking invisible aid.

"Claudia, listen to me—is there an intercom in here? A speaker of some kind? The voice has to be rigged some way—it's not really your mother—Claudia!"

But Claudia was doubled over, clutching her stomach, her face a blank white mask. Robin ran to her, eased the girl down onto the floor, and shook her by the shoulders.

"Claudia—listen to me! Someone's trying to hurt you—someone's trying to make you *think* your mother is after you! Do you understand?

They're trying to make you *think* you're crazy, but you're *not!*"

The girl's eyes were glazed and empty.

"Can you hear me?" Robin patted Claudia's hands, chafed her wrists, babbling to her the whole time. "I think it's Parker, Claudia—I think it's Parker doing all those horrible things. I told the police about it—maybe I shouldn't have, but I *had* to do something—and I told Walt, too—"

She broke off, fighting tears. "Oh, Claudia . . ."

Robin looked deep into the girl's eyes, but all she could see was her own hazy reflection surrounded by despair.

"Claudia," Robin whispered, "I'm not going to let them hurt you! I'm not going to let anything happen to you. I'm going to get you out of here. Come on—you're going home with me."

She managed to stand the girl up and turn her in the opposite direction. But as they took a step into the hall, something exploded behind them with such force that a wet spray of glass and splinters seemed to fill the room.

Claudia shrieked and covered her head with her arms, and at the same time Robin shoved the girl up against the corridor wall.

"Don't move!" Robin ordered her.

Alarmed, she raced back into the study. She could see the broken window by the desk, and the shards of shattered glass everywhere, and the torrents of rain pouring in, soaking everything in proximity. Her first thought was that someone had deliberately thrown something through the windowpane, but then she saw the huge tree limb showing through the wall, and she actually felt relieved.

"It's okay!" she called, turning back. "The storm must have uprooted a tree!"

She stepped on something squishy.

Horror-stricken, she looked down and saw the disembodied hand lying on the floor beneath her shoe.

Robin kicked the thing away, and yet still she stood there watching it, mesmerized somehow, as if she half expected the hand to come crawling back after her and clamp on to her ankle. And suddenly she could feel every instinct screaming within her—every nerve—every feeling in her whole body screaming at her—*Run! Run!* Slowly she inched toward the door, and then she made a bolt for the hallway, her only thought to get back to Claudia.

"Come on, Claudia—we're going—"

Robin stopped, her words frozen on her lips.

The corridor was empty.

Claudia was gone.

For one second of sheer panic, Robin didn't know what to do. She stood there gazing stupidly at the spot where Claudia had been, and from some remote corner of her mind she felt her feet moving her back toward the study, back to where she knew there was a telephone and a line to help. . . .

Robin's head came up and her body went rigid. Somewhere in the house a door slammed.

It was a distant, muffled sound, buried beneath the wailing of the storm outside, but at the same instant she'd heard it, Robin had also heard something else.

A faint, brief cry.

Claudia calling for help?

It was enough to spur Robin to action.

She made her way fearfully along the hall. Again she heard the muffled slamming sound— and then again. As she came upon the arched threshold near the front of the passageway, a rush of damp air swirled out to meet her, and Robin realized she was just outside the room where she'd first met Mr. Swanson and talked about her job. *Only a few nights ago . . . it seems like forever. . . .*

The banging came again . . . louder now . . . more insistent.

The French doors, Robin thought suddenly.

Claudia came this way. Whoever took Claudia brought her here and out again through the French doors.

Robin hurried into the room, her heart quickening. Two of the tall doors hadn't been fastened, and as the wind tore at them, they swung back and forth against the wall. Robin slipped between them and shut them firmly behind her.

It was gushing rain now.

As she stood there in despair and looked helplessly around her, all she could see was an endless tangle of trees and heavy mist and shadows. *They've gone into the woods. . . . I'll never find her now. . . .*

But she had to try.

She knew she'd never forgive herself if she didn't.

"Claudia!" she screamed.

The wind lashed her words away, as though she'd never screamed at all.

Robin stared at the twisted trees until she finally spotted a wide space off to one side. *There . . . they must have gone through there.* She pushed her wet hair from her face and ran for the opening.

The forest seemed to swallow her. As Robin pushed her way through a maze of trunks and branches, she didn't even notice the scratches on her face, the limbs tearing at her hair. Her jacket ripped, but she didn't hear; she felt blood on her lips and licked it away without realizing.

She pressed deeper and deeper into the woods. She forgot about the hidden holes, the sudden ditches and gulleys, the deceptive drifts of old, wet leaves. More than once she stumbled and pitched forward, scraping her hands, tearing her jeans, only to get up, catch her breath, and go on again. The ground was growing soggier—in most places the mud was up to her ankles now. It sucked at her, trying to drag her down, and just as she was about to give up in despair, she saw something in the path and stopped to pick it up.

Claudia's shoe.

"Claudia!" she screamed again. "Where are you?"

But of course Claudia wouldn't answer . . . she *couldn't* answer.

She'll be so terrified by now . . . if she isn't already dead—

"No," Robin said savagely to herself, and she bit her lip, tasting salty tears and blood. "No, no, no!"

A fierce anger filled her, and she plunged on through the woods. The rain was coming down in buckets.

Robin had no idea where she was or how far she'd even come. She only knew that she had to find Claudia before it was too late.

"Claudia!" Robin shouted. "Where are you?"

And then she froze.

Through the thick gray gloom of the forest, she saw a shadow standing straight ahead of her . . . a tall silent statue among the trees.

She saw it for only a second—saw its dark, indistinct shape—yet she knew it was human.

And that it was watching her.

Robin's feet wouldn't move.

Her brain whirled, and she reached out for the nearest tree trunk to hold herself steady. She willed herself to go on, and as she began to plod forward again, the figure vanished into the fog.

I imagined it . . . I probably only imagined it. . . .

Without warning her foot snagged, and she

hurtled through the air, landing several feet away in the mud. She tried to get up but couldn't. She tried again but only slipped deeper into the muck. Twisting around, she spotted a fallen tree branch she thought she could use to boost herself back up. She reached out for it, groping clumsily through a soggy pile of leaves and mud.

Her fingers closed around something soft.

As her grip tightened, the thing seemed to pop softly within her hand and burst and slowly melt.

Startled, Robin pushed the hair back from her eyes so she could get a better look.

She stared down at the thing in her hand.

Stared . . .

And stared . . .

She saw the stump of the arm . . . and the rotting torso, all covered with greenish slime . . .

And as she felt bile come up in her own throat, she saw the maggots swarming over Vicki Hastings's mutilated face.

18

She's pretty, ain't she?" the voice said above her, and Robin rolled over with a scream.

"Real pretty." Roy Skaggs stepped out of the trees, grinning, his arms folded across his chest.

Robin couldn't speak. She only stared at the tall figure towering above her and kept sliding backward through the mud, trying to get away from him.

"You're gonna look just like her." His grin widened. "All nice and soft and tender to touch . . . just like girls are supposed to be, right?"

He made a move as though he would lean over to touch her, and Robin scooted out of his reach. She thought he might have laughed softly, deep, deep in his throat.

"Only one difference." Skaggs shook his head, taking another step closer. "I didn't *mean* to hurt her. But I mean to *kill* you."

He uncrossed his arms.

He had something in his hand, and as Robin stared, he held it out tantalizingly, over her head.

"See here?"

She could see. It was the photograph of herself, the one missing from the school bulletin board, and as she stared at it, Skaggs took a lighter from his pocket and held it to one corner of the picture. It hissed and curled, and a thin stream of smoke wafted up into the air as her photo face bubbled and blackened.

"All gone," Skaggs said softly. "All . . . gone."

Robin's mind was spinning so fast, the world turned black around her.

"You . . ." she mumbled. "I don't understand —where's Claudia?"

"Claudia?" He frowned and rubbed his chin with one filthy hand. "Claudia . . . hmmm . . . poor little helpless Claudia . . . Poor crazy little thing." He slapped one hand against his thigh and faked surprise. "Why, I don't know! Maybe you better ask my boss!"

"Boss?" And Robin could see his lips spread apart in a sleazy grin, and the thunder rumbled overhead, as deep and dangerous as the laugh in Skaggs's chest.

"Why, sure." Skaggs took a step toward her and prodded her with the toe of his muddy boot. "My boss. But, wait. You wanna see Claudia? Then I'll take you to see Claudia!"

"What have you done to her? No!" Once more

Robin tried to scoot away from him, but this time he grabbed her and yanked her to her feet.

"In fact, I'll take you right now, whatcha say?"

He was laughing and laughing, and as Robin screamed and tried to break away, he pinned her arms behind her back with a grip of steel. He half dragged, half carried her through the woods, and as they came out into a small clearing, Robin saw a wooden shack ahead of them cleverly camouflaged by the surrounding trees.

"Won't you come in?" Skaggs laughed, and with one thrust he flung Robin through the open doorway. She skidded hard across the floor and slammed into a corner, lying there dazed while Skaggs shut the door and stood over her.

The room spun crazily. It took Robin several seconds to fight off the dizziness, and as she did so, the contents of the shelves around her—shovels, hoes and spades, clippers and pointed shears—came slowly and unsteadily into focus.

"Where's Claudia?" she mumbled. "What have you done with her?"

"Why, haven't you heard?" Skaggs put his hands on his head and widened his eyes. "She's insane!"

Robin pulled her legs up to her chest, as if she could huddle herself into an invisible ball. Skaggs reached down and ran one hand slowly across her head.

"Nice girl. Nice . . . little girl." He grinned. "Nice you could drop in and see me today. But hey—sorry. Gotta go. You have an appointment with an accident."

Robin stared at him through a haze of confusion and terror. She could see his narrowed eyes inspecting her, going slowly over her body, and suddenly he squatted down on his heels beside her.

"You know . . . I was just thinkin'," he said, and he put his hand on her shoulder. "There might still be time for you and me to be friends. Before you have to go. What do you think—you like that idea?"

Robin shoved out at him. Her sudden movement caught him off guard, and he tumbled back onto the floor. As she flattened herself into her corner, he staggered clumsily to his feet and yanked his shirt halfway open.

"You shouldn't have done that. That other one—she did that, too—tried to get rough with me. And I took care of her—I took real good care of her."

"You took her picture down, didn't you?" Robin murmured, and she saw the slow, pleased nod of his head.

"My collection." Skaggs grinned. "She was my first. But you know what they say about hobbies . . . once you start, it's so easy to get hooked." His shoulders shook in a silent laugh, and his eyes gleamed at her through the shadows.

"Where's Claudia!" Robin screamed at him.

"I like the feel of it now. The feel of soft, bare skin . . . and cold, hard fear . . ."

"Where is she!"

"Well, we're not gonna worry about her right now. We're gonna worry about you. 'Cause you're gonna be next. And you know what? I think I like you even better . . ."

Skaggs gave a fiendish grin. He reached inside his shirt and slowly pulled out a knife.

"No," Robin whispered. "Oh, God, please help me. . . ."

And then she noticed the figure in the doorway.

It was silhouetted there against the raging storm, and in the dim light of the cabin, it seemed just another shadow, hazy and indistinct. Robin's heart leapt into her throat, and her eyes went wide. She hadn't heard it come—didn't know how long it had even been there—but as Skaggs took a step toward her, the shadow moved stealthily along one of the shelves and floated up behind him.

"You might as well relax"—Skaggs grinned—"and enjoy it."

He knelt down beside her.

He held the tip of the blade to her throat and leaned in close to her neck.

Robin could smell his foul breath.

She could feel his hand on her jacket, and the zipper starting down.

She heard his laugh . . .

And then she heard his scream.

The knife grazed the side of her neck as Skaggs made a horrible choking sound . . .

And as his whole body went suddenly rigid, he fell on top of Robin, pinning her to the floor.

19

"Robin!" Claudia cried. "Are you all right?"

And someone was pulling on Skaggs, pulling at his heavy, twisted body, trying to get Robin free—

"Robin—oh, Robin—"

"Claudia," Robin murmured. "What are you —how—"

"Please get up, Robin! Did he hurt you?"

At last Robin was able to roll out from under Skaggs's weight, and as she stumbled to her feet, Claudia threw her arms around her, hugging her tightly.

"I thought you were dead," Claudia said tearfully.

"I thought you were, too!" Still somewhat dazed, Robin clung to her. "But what happened? Are *you* all right?"

"Yes, but . . ."

As Robin pulled away and held her at arm's length, Claudia stared down at the body on the floor. She stared and she stared, and as her eyes slowly began to widen, she pressed her hands to her mouth and swallowed a sob.

"Oh, my God," Claudia whispered. "Oh, my God, what have I done?"

Robin grabbed her arm and pulled her toward the doorway. "You had to do it, Claudia—you didn't have any choice! You were only trying to save me!"

But Claudia's horrified gaze was fixed on Skaggs, and without warning she reeled into a corner and got sick.

Robin watched her helplessly and then turned her attention back to the body. He was twisted at a crazy angle, and a pair of shears protruded from his back, propping him off the floor as if he were still trying to struggle to his feet.

Robin felt as if she might be sick herself. She swallowed hard and reached out for Claudia, pulling her gently back to the doorway.

"Come on, we've got to get the police."

"We've got to hurry," Claudia said softly, and her eyes had that distant clouded look again that Robin had come to recognize. Quickly Robin grabbed the girl and shook her roughly by the shoulders.

"Claudia, you've got to tell me what happened," she insisted. "Where were you? What happened back there in the house?"

"We've got to hurry," Claudia monotoned again, and as her eyes reluctantly drew back to Skaggs's lifeless figure, Robin shook her again.

"Claudia!"

"Yes . . . yes . . ." Claudia's brow furrowed, as if she were finding it too difficult to remember. "He'll be back soon. We can't let him find us here."

"Who'll be back?" Robin demanded. "Talk to me, Claudia!"

"You were right, Robin. I didn't want to believe you, but . . ." Claudia's eyes lifted, filmy with tears. "You were right about Parker. Only he's been using Skaggs to do most of the work."

"Skaggs . . ." Robin turned loose of her and took a step back, shaking her head in amazement. "Skaggs."

It made perfect sense, of course. Skaggs at school, having access to the locker rooms, the showers . . . He'd know locker combinations, too, or he'd know where to find them—it'd be easy for him to slip threatening notes into someone's books . . . to push someone down the stairs and slip quickly out of sight into some empty room or some closet . . .

"So easy," Robin mumbled. "So simple and so easy."

Skaggs could drive a black car, and Skaggs would have access to Manorwood. He'd worked the property for years—he'd know all about the house, where to turn the electricity on and off. It'd be easy for him to rig up a floating body in the storage room using Winifred's curtains . . . and Parker had covered for him perfectly.

"He used the flashlight, so I couldn't really see the floor," Robin mumbled. "If the lights had been on, I'd probably have noticed the floor was still wet, but in the dark I couldn't tell."

"What?" Claudia seemed to rouse herself. She wiped at her tears and looked blankly at Robin.

"Don't you see, Claudia? It was there all the time, and we never even guessed! Parker and Skaggs made the perfect team."

Parker had even admitted to Robin that he knew where she lived . . . so he wouldn't have had any trouble leaving the note on her door that night . . . or sending Skaggs to do it. . . .

"We've got to go," Claudia said again, breaking into Robin's thoughts. "When he comes back and finds what's happened—"

"Who?" Robin reached out for her, but Claudia's arms were wrapped tightly around herself and she was trembling.

"When . . . when Skaggs brought me here," Claudia whispered, "Parker was waiting in the woods. He—he told Skaggs to take care of what had to be done. And that . . . that he would be back later. After it was over."

Robin stared. She felt strangely frozen and faraway.

"I saw him leave the house as I was coming in," she said. "He was in a real hurry."

The air was thick with danger. Claudia put one hand out behind her, groping for the door.

"Come on," Robin whispered, but Claudia shook her head.

"What are we going to do with him? When Parker comes back, he'll find him here."

"It doesn't matter," Robin insisted. "We're going to the police. It doesn't matter if we leave him or not."

Claudia couldn't seem to stop shaking. Her voice quivered so violently, she could hardly speak.

"It—it does matter. Don't you see? If the police—if the police don't believe us about Parker—then—then—they'll see Skaggs and we're—*I'm*—the one who killed him!"

Robin felt her heart go cold. *Yes, he planned it. He planned it right down to the last detail. Drive Claudia crazy . . . no one's going to believe that Parker Swanson could ever be mixed up in something sordid or messy. "He's brilliant . . . has the brains . . . knows how to work people . . . that's how you survive . . ."*

And Claudia will be gotten rid of after all.

"Crazy old Claudia . . ."

"We need to wipe off the fingerprints," Robin said dully. Her voice sounded foreign to her, and very faraway. She stared at the shears sticking out of Skaggs's back, and then she stared at Claudia.

Claudia looked horrified. "I . . . I can't touch them."

Robin glanced wildly around the room.

"We'll hide him," she said.

"What?"

"At least till I can talk to Walt." *Yes, Walt.* He knew everything that had been going on—he'd know what to do.

"Oh, Robin, we can't!" Claudia went paler, but Robin shook her head and took a step toward the body.

"Just till I can find out what to do!" she said, more sharply than she intended.

It seemed an eternity that Claudia stood there, gazing down at the pool of blood spreading out from beneath Skaggs . . . the thick dark stain spreading out across the dirty floor. Finally she whispered, "I know someplace," and reached out to squeeze Robin's hand.

Robin thought she would faint when she had to touch him.

As she tried to lift his legs up, Skaggs flopped sideways, and she gave a cry and jumped back.

"That thing's sticking out of his back—we can't lay him down," Claudia said, her voice lifting shrilly, and Robin nodded.

"You're right. We'll have to drag him this way. On his face."

She could see the shears buried clear up to their handles, and she wondered how Claudia had ever found the strength to plunge them in. Fighting down a wave of nausea, she worked her way around to Skaggs's other end and wrestled his limp arms above his head. Claudia groaned and got hold of his boots.

"What about the blood?" she whispered.

Robin straightened up again, one hand to her

forehead, trying to think. Quickly she scanned the room, but there was nothing they could use to wipe up the floor.

"Here," Robin said and began pulling off her sweater.

Claudia looked at her, horrified. "What do you think you're doing? Put that back on!"

"We've got to do *something!*" Before Claudia could say anything more, Robin dropped to her knees, pressing her sweater into the growing puddle.

"Then put on my sweatshirt." Claudia peeled it off and handed it to Robin, even as Robin was trying to push it back at her.

"Forget it! You'll catch pneumonia!"

"Not any more than you will!" Claudia insisted. "And I have a flannel shirt on underneath —you've only got a T-shirt."

Nodding, Robin took the sweatshirt and wriggled into it. As she scrubbed fiercely at the floorboards, she watched the dark red stains soak into her favorite sweater and tried not to gag.

"Okay?" Claudia asked at last.

Again Robin nodded, holding out the soggy sweater. "What do we do with this?"

"Tie it around his neck."

Together they knotted the sleeves around Skaggs's neck, then repositioned themselves at each end of his body.

Then they pulled.

At some point Robin actually felt her mind blanking out. Mercifully, she felt herself moving through a kind of numbing fog, rain gushing down all around her, the forest enclosing her, protecting her, hiding her darkest secrets. It took forever to move Skaggs from the shack and through the trees. Once Claudia stumbled and fell on top of him, and as she gave way to hysteria, Robin slammed back to consciousness and held the girl until Claudia could calm down again.

"Where is this place?" Robin asked wearily. She was soaked through and drenched in mud and chilled to her very soul. To her immense relief, Claudia pointed toward a break in the trees.

"There."

She looked like a drowned little mouse, Robin thought, tiny and helpless and utterly terrified. Robin gathered her own last ounce of strength and hauled the body several more yards, falling gratefully out into another small clearing.

They were standing on a ledge. Robin could see bare treetops clawing their way up a craggy incline below them, and from somewhere beneath the pouring rain came a distant sound of rushing water.

Claudia sank down onto the ground to catch her breath. Robin's eyes swept over the edge of the precipice and focused on the twisted riverbed far, far below, its banks swirling with rainwater now, its boundaries marked by clusters of jagged rocks.

It was a sheer drop.

"We can't," Robin murmured. "We can't put him there."

She turned back around. Claudia was rocking slowly back and forth . . . back and forth . . . and seemed to be talking quietly to herself.

"Claudia," Robin said again, louder this time, "we can't put Skaggs down there."

Claudia stared at her.

She got unsteadily to her feet, and her eyes were huge and frightened.

"What are we going to do, Robin?"

"I don't know." Robin shook her head, and as Claudia came over to her, she put her arms around the girl and held her tightly.

"I'm scared," Claudia whispered.

"So am I. But I just can't do this. Skaggs can't go down there."

"You're right," Claudia said softly, and she pulled back and touched Robin gently on the cheek. "You go instead."

20

A strange sense of unreality settled over Robin.

She felt the pounding rain and the icy wind, and as she stared into Claudia's huge eyes, she thought there might have been a faint flicker of triumph somewhere in all that emptiness.

"I have this," Claudia said quietly. "It belongs to Parker, but I know how to use it."

Her arms were still around Robin. Only now Robin felt something hard and sharp pressed into her back, and as Claudia released her, Robin saw the gun in Claudia's hand.

"You made it so easy for me," Claudia said, and her tone held a note of wonder. "I set it up so carefully . . . and then *you* came along and made the whole thing work. Even better than I could ever have hoped."

"Claudia," Robin murmured, "I don't under-stand—"

"But it's so simple, Robin. Just like me." And Claudia smiled a strange smile. "Simple . . . crazy . . . Claudia."

Robin moved forward, but the gun came up in her face.

"No, Robin. Wrong way."

"Let's just go back to the house, Claudia. You and I together. We could—"

"The only place you're going is down."

The gun came closer. Robin took one step back, glancing fearfully over her shoulder at the long, sheer drop.

"It's nothing personal, really," Claudia went on, her eyes going slowly from Robin's head to her feet. "It's the family I'm after. But to hurt them, I have to hurt Parker. And to hurt Parker, I have to hurt you."

"What are you talking about?" Robin's voice rose. "I don't mean anything to Parker—"

"Actually, you're going to end up meaning quite a lot." Claudia nodded. "Because when they find *you,* and you're wearing *my* sweatshirt, they're going to think Parker was after *me* but got *you* by mistake."

Robin stared at her. She could hear Claudia talking, could see Claudia's lips moving, but the words seemed very foreign and very far away.

"You . . . you mean . . . they'll think Parker tried . . . to kill you."

"They might think that." Claudia nodded. "Or they might think I finally decided to jump. I'm very unstable, you know. Suicidal. I could snap at any time."

A crash of thunder sounded overhead. The ground trembled beneath their feet, and the rain beat down like pellets.

"Either way, Parker's to blame, isn't he?" Claudia went on calmly. "Either way, he's already a suspect. You did that for me, Robin. I have you to thank for that bit of luck."

Robin felt sick inside. She closed her eyes for a brief instant, willing herself not to swoon.

"You even told the police." Claudia smiled. "So who do you suppose they'll think of first when they find you dead?"

"You really hate him, don't you?" Robin said. "Even though he's never done anything to you."

To her dismay, Claudia laughed a soft laugh.

"No, Robin, I told you before, it's nothing that personal. I just know that by destroying Parker, it's the worst thing I could ever do to this family."

Again the gun came closer. Robin could smell the cold tang of steel beside her cheek.

"Parker's their hope, you know—or haven't you heard? Parker's their pride and joy. But now Parker won't have his money—I will. Or his freedom, but I will. And the Swansons, bless their cold hearts, won't have their perfect family name anymore."

Claudia gazed a long moment into Robin's face. Her eyes brightened with quick tears, and they seemed to grow, pools of deep, deep sadness. Robin wanted to look away from them but found she couldn't.

"I want him to suffer," Claudia whispered. "And if *he* suffers, they all suffer. Just like my mother suffered every single day after she married into this family."

Robin's only thought was to keep Claudia talking. *Yes, keep her talking . . . distract her . . .*

"But I thought Parker's father loved her," Robin said. "I thought—"

"The old man always hated my mother." Claudia's face went dark. "And so did Parker. They talked about her behind her back, but she knew. She always knew. When they called her a phony and a fraud. When they said she used people."

Claudia gave a short, bitter laugh.

"Can you imagine that—my mother using people! Well, people *liked* to have my mother love them! She was a very beautiful woman, you know. Even me . . ."

Her voice trailed off. A look of confusion flickered across her face, and she seemed to lose her train of thought.

"Even . . . even me," Claudia said at last. "I worked hard to make my mother happy. To make her . . . love me."

The gun tightened against Robin's face. She stiffened slowly, feeling the rain flow down her cheeks.

"I . . . I worked hard," Claudia mumbled. "I did a lot to earn my mother's love. I even got rid of Parker's mother to make my mother happy."

Robin gasped, but Claudia didn't seem to hear. Her face had gone soft and dreamy, as though she were far away in some other place.

"I knew my mother wanted to be a Swanson," Claudia mumbled. "More than anything in the world. And so"—she closed her eyes and drew a long, deep breath—"that day . . . when Mrs. Swanson drove to the village . . . I waited on the curve. And when I saw her car . . . I stepped out in front of it."

Robin tried to block out the sound of Claudia's memories, tried desperately to shut out the horrible tragedy tearing at her heart as Claudia kept on.

"I knew she wouldn't hit me. She was a very sweet person . . . a very kind person. And she did just what I knew she'd do. She swerved her car over the ledge, and it went down and down and down . . ."

Claudia's lip trembled. Her voice was thick with tears.

"Everyone said it was an accident. But somehow . . . I think Parker always suspected."

She sighed, her voice dropping to a whisper.

"I did a lot for my mother, you see. And now I'm doing this for her, too."

"Claudia," Robin begged, "think about what'll happen. Sooner or later they'll know it was you—they'll find you and they'll lock you away, and you know how much you'll hate that—"

"But they won't know," Claudia looked slightly bewildered. "How could they ever know? You'll be gone . . . and Skaggs—"

"They'll think it's strange when they find both of us down there—they'll never believe that both of us fell—"

"But they won't find both of you," Claudia said patiently, as though she were speaking to a slow child. "Don't you see? I'm going to bury Skaggs in the woods. I only needed help getting him here. I was going to kill him anyway, but again, you made it so easy for me. The shears were a nice touch, don't you think? If I'd used the gun, I would've given myself away."

"Someone at school will notice he's gone," Robin reminded her. "And everyone knows he works for you. They'll find him sooner or later."

Claudia shook her head. "And everyone knows what he is, Robin. An irresponsible drunk. And if he suddenly stops showing up for work here, too, do you think anyone's going to drag us in for questioning?" Her lips moved in a cold, humorless smile. "Manorwood is a very big place. You can hide things here for a very long time."

"Like Vicki?" Robin's voice shook.

"That wasn't my fault," Claudia said softly, and she glanced away. "I don't think Skaggs really meant to kill her. But she was trespassing that night, and he was drunk. I was coming up the drive when I thought I heard screaming—but I got there too late. And so"—she inclined her head—"Skaggs and I made a deal."

"I was almost right, wasn't I?" Robin stared at her. "Only it was *you* he was working for, not Parker."

"I needed help with my little plan," Claudia said evenly. "And Skaggs needed his secret kept."

Robin nodded slowly. The terrible fear she'd felt all this time was slowly draining now . . . replaced by a cold, hollow disgust.

"There's only one thing I can't figure out," she said.

"What's that?"

"The voice. Your poor dead mother calling for help. It couldn't have been Skaggs every time."

Again that strange, vague smile touched Claudia's face.

"A little something I inherited from her. Lillith . . . medium extraordinaire." She gave a sharp laugh. "Of course she was a fraud . . . and she taught me well."

Claudia tilted her face to one side. To Robin's shock, an eerie voice called out through the rain, floating from nowhere, and yet everywhere . . .

"Help . . . help me . . ."

"It's called throwing your voice, Robin. It's a trick all good mediums know how to do."

"My God, Claudia," Robin whispered, and she held her eyes steady on Claudia's vacant stare. "You really are insane—"

"Don't you say that!" Claudia screamed.

To Robin's horror the gun dug into her cheek. She could see Claudia's eyes, wide and wild, and the gun, like Claudia's voice, was trembling violently.

"Don't you ever say that to me!" Claudia screamed again. "My *mother* was insane! *Lillith* was insane! I'm not *like* her! I was *never* like her!"

Terrified, Robin felt Claudia crowd against her. She felt her foot slide in the mud . . . felt part of the ground dissolve beneath her shoe.

"Don't do this, Claudia," she begged. "Please . . ."

"I *have* to do it!" Claudia cried. "I have to do it for my mother! Don't you understand, they ruined her *life!* She *killed* herself because of them!"

"You're wrong, Claudia," said a familiar voice. "*I* killed her."

21

As Claudia whirled around, a thin shadow emerged slowly through the trees, shrouded in the foggy downpour.

Winifred stopped several yards away and looked at them.

"I killed your mother," she said calmly. "There was no one else but me."

Claudia spun back toward Robin, the gun quivering wildly in her hand.

"You're *lying! They* made her do it! They *drove* her to it!"

Winifred shook her head. "They didn't even know."

"They hated her, and—and—"

"Don't you mean," Winifred corrected gently, *"she* hated *them?* She's the one who despised their happiness. She's the one who wanted to break them apart."

"I—I—" Claudia clamped her other hand on the gun now, both arms stretched in front of her. "I don't believe you! They wanted to hurt her, and they did!"

"They wanted to *help* her, but she wouldn't be helped. They wanted to *love* her, but she preferred to take advantage of their kindness. I couldn't let her do that. I couldn't let her hurt my family. So one night I brought her her usual dose of sleeping pills. Only I brought it a little early, in her dinner wine. And then I waited for her to go for her walk, which she always did right after dark. And then I followed her."

Winifred paused to take a deep breath. When she continued, her voice was steady and matter-of-fact.

"It was raining that night—it got much worse while we were out. I made sure she didn't suffer. It was very quick and very merciful. There was very little pain. I put the razor in her own hands. I helped her, very gently, to make the incisions—"

"No!" Claudia shouted. "I'm not going to listen to this!"

"It began to rain much harder, and she began to grow much weaker. I simply coaxed her forward, over the edge of the cliff."

"No!"

Winifred folded her hands at her waist. "So you see, Claudia . . . all this has been for nothing."

The gun barrel struck Robin so fast she didn't

even see it coming. She only felt the crack on her skull and the ground dissolving beneath her feet as she toppled back into nothingness.

She grabbed for Claudia on the way down.

She felt Claudia's leg clutched in her arms . . . felt Claudia's body twisting as it slid closer and closer to the edge of the precipice. Robin hung there, suspended, and screamed.

Claudia kicked out at her. Robin tightened her hold on Claudia's thigh and groped out frantically with her own foot, trying to find a niche in the slippery wall of rock.

"Robin!" someone shouted.

Her muscles were on fire. She felt herself weakening, and as Claudia jerked sideways, Robin slid several inches lower.

"Help me!" she screamed again.

She could feel something happening— movement and tension above her. Her body swung hard into the rocks, scraping and sliding on its way up. And then suddenly there were arms reaching, hands pulling, someone grabbing her legs and her clothes, pulling her from Claudia—

For one quick moment she saw Walt's strained face leaning over her, but then, as something moved at her side, she saw Claudia's body disappearing over the edge of the cliff.

"Claudia!" Robin lunged for her, but Parker was faster. As the girl's hands gripped the edge of the rock, Parker stared at them with a look of pure hatred.

"No," Robin begged him. "Parker—don't!"

"Don't do it, man," Walt said.

Parker seemed to freeze.

He stared down at the water far, far below.

"No," Robin whispered. "Parker . . ."

Parker's face twisted.

Bracing himself, he groaned and tried to pull Claudia back.

For a moment she hung there . . . a pale delicate feather in the storm.

And then she smiled.

Robin saw her jerk free. And as Claudia hurtled down to the rocks, Robin pressed her head against Walt's shoulder to shut out the wail of the wind.

22

"**A**re the police finally gone?" Herk asked, peeking cautiously into the living room. When only three faces nodded back at him, he shuffled in, relieved. "I thought they'd never get out of here with all their questions. Don't they care I'm an old man and need some peace? Don't they think we've had enough trouble here for one day?"

He looks pale, Robin thought from her place on the couch. *He never seemed frail to me before, but tonight . . .*

"No more police." Herk sighed. "If a cop comes to the door, just run him right off. Got that?"

Rousing herself, Robin turned her attention from Herk and shot Walt an accusing look.

"And to think you told me not to even *go* to the police."

"A lot of good that did me," Walt replied.

"Well, *you* went to the police," she persisted.

"We went to the police," Walt corrected her, glancing over at Parker. "After Parker found Vicki's body out in the woods, he called me and we started putting two and two together. Going to the police seemed like a good thing to do."

"But you *suspected* Parker!" Robin pulled the blanket tighter around her shoulders and scooted closer to the blazing fire. "Did Walt tell you he suspected you?" she added stubbornly to Parker.

The boys exchanged amused looks.

"I never said that." Walt shook his head. "I said I was speculating."

"I told the police, but they wouldn't believe me," Robin pushed her muddy hair back from her forehead and frowned. "If they'd believed me, none of this might have happened in the first place. Why did they believe you and not me?"

"Because I happen to have an in," Walt said smoothly.

"Your uncle." Robin sighed. "Of course, I should have remembered. That's not fair."

"Fair or not, I knew the cops would believe him long before they'd believe the crazy story *you* were going to tell them."

"It doesn't matter who went," Parker broke in. "I'm just glad we got back here when we did." He glanced over at Robin's disheveled appearance and hid a smile. "What a picture of beauty. Kind of makes you wonder if it was really worth rescuing her, doesn't it?"

He grinned then as Robin burrowed self-consciously into her blanket.

"This job is too much for me, Herk." She sighed. "I'm retiring."

"Retirement not accepted," Herk barked. "Need to see more of you. Livens the place up."

"Livens the place up?" Parker echoed. "I think I liked it better dull."

"You're the only dull thing around here!" Herk snorted. "And as for those books," he went on, turning back to Robin, "tomorrow they go to the library—lock, stock, and barrel—just as they are! I'll think of something else for you to do! You can be my companion—how about that?"

"Hmmm . . ." Robin smiled. "That's certainly a job worth considering."

"You bet it is," Herk agreed.

For a while the room lapsed into silence. Rain beat against the windowpanes, and the fire crackled softly on the hearth.

Robin lowered her head onto her arms and stared numbly into the flames. *We're trying to act so normal . . . trying to laugh . . . make jokes . . . not think . . . forget.* It had been a long, exhausting day, and she felt drained and detached, as though everything had been part of some terrible nightmare.

"What will happen to Winifred?" she murmured.

Looking up, she saw that Parker and Walt and even Herk were all staring at her. From the grave expressions on their faces, she knew they'd been sharing her same thoughts.

"We'll get her a good lawyer, of course." Herk stabbed a poker viciously at the fire, but Robin heard the quiver in his voice. "The best. After all, she's just like family, isn't she. She's . . ."

His voice trailed off. He stared solemnly into the flames, and Robin's heart ached for him . . . for Winifred . . . for every innocent victim of every human tragedy.

"Well," Walt said, deliberately breaking the silence. He stood up and glanced over at Robin. "Can I give anyone a ride home?"

"I can take her." Parker got up and looked at Walt.

"But you're already home," Walt pointed out politely. "And her house is right on my way."

"If I'd known you were going to give me all this competition," Parker deadpanned, "I'd never have confided in you this morning."

"You're right. You should have just kept quiet and let her be terrorized," Walt agreed.

"You both lose," Herk spoke up. "I'm taking Robin out tonight."

"You are?" Robin looked surprised.

"You betcha. That brand-new pizza place I keep hearing about. Want to boogie. Might even sing with the band."

Parker stared. "Are you serious?"

"Of course I'm not serious, you imbecile!" Herk shuffled back toward the hallway. "The only date *I* have is with my pillow! And if you two know what's good for you, you'll take Robin Bailey out somewhere nice and treat her like the sweet, special girl she is, and help her forget all about this terrible day she'd never have had if she hadn't answered that ad!"

"Well, it was your idea," Parker reminded him.

"I know it was my idea," his grandfather snapped, turning in the doorway to give Robin a sly wink. "And it might interest you to know that in spite of everything, I'm *glad* she answered it! So what do you think about that?"

"I think it's time to go eat," Walt said diplomatically, reaching for Robin's hand, helping her up from the couch. "What do *you* think, Robin?"

Robin looked at the floor. She thought about how impossible this would all sound when she tried to explain it to her mother tonight. She thought about how dramatic Faye would be when she found out about Robin's weekend. She thought about all the gossip and rumors and questions that would be waiting for her at school Monday morning, and how nice and normal everything had been before—

Before? Was that only a few days ago?

And it came to her with a sudden shock that her life—and her self—would never be quite the same, ever again.

"Robin?" Walt asked gently, still holding her hand.

"You okay?" Parker reached over and squeezed her shoulder.

"Me?" Robin glanced up, embarrassed by their stares. "Oh, sure. Just lead me on to the next big adventure."

"I'll do the leading," Parker said firmly.

"I'm already leading," Walt reminded him, pulling Robin out into the hall.

"In case you two haven't noticed," Robin broke in, flustered, "I'm perfectly capable of handling things by myself."

The boys stopped in their tracks.

They looked down at Robin, and then they grinned.

"Well . . . *almost,*" Parker said.

"With a *little* help from your backup," Walt clarified.

Robin felt her cheeks burn, a warm glow that spread deep inside her.

Maybe some of these new changes in her life weren't going to be so bad after all.

About the Author

Richie Tankersley Cusick loves to read and write scary books. Richie enjoys writing when it is rainy and gloomy outside, and likes to have a spooky soundtrack playing in the background. She writes at a desk that originally belonged to a funeral director in the 1800s and that she believes is haunted. Halloween is one of her favorite holidays. She and her husband decorate the entire house, which includes having a body laid out in state in the parlor, lifesize models of Frankenstein's monster, the figure of Death to keep watch, and a scary costume for Hannah, their dog. A neighbor recently told them that a previous owner of the house was feared by all of the neighborhood kids and no one would go to the house on Halloween.

Richie is the author of *Vampire, Fatal Secrets, The Mall, Silent Stalker, Help Wanted,* and the novelization of *Buffy, the Vampire Slayer.* She and her husband, Rick, live outside Kansas City, where she is currently at work on her next novel.